PEW

ALSO BY CATHERINE LACEY

Nobody Is Ever Missing

The Answers

Certain American States

PEW

CATHERINE LACEY

GRANTA

Granta Publications, 12 Addison Avenue, London W11 4QR

First published in Great Britain by Granta Books, 2020
First published in the United States in 2020 by Farrar, Straus and Giroux, New York.

A CIP catalogue record for this book is available from the British Library.

3 5 7 9 10 8 6 4 2

ISBN 978 1 78378 517 9
eISBN 978 1 78378 518 6

Offset by Avon DataSet Ltd, 4 Arden Court, Arden Road, Alcester, Warwickshire
B49 6HN
Printed and bound by CPI Group (UK) Ltd, Croydon, CR0 4YY
www.granta.com

For Jesse Ball

These people go out into the street, and walk down the street alone. They keep walking, and walk straight out of the city of Omelas, through the beautiful gates. They keep walking across the farmlands of Omelas. Each one goes alone, youth or girl, man or woman. Night falls; the traveler must pass down village streets, between the houses with yellow-lit windows, and on out into the darkness of the fields. Each alone, they go west or north, towards the mountains. They go on. They leave Omelas, they walk ahead into the darkness, and they do not come back. The place they go towards is a place even less imaginable to most of us than the city of happiness. I cannot describe it at all. It is possible that it does not exist. But they seem to know where they are going, the ones who walk away from Omelas.

—"The Ones Who Walk Away from Omelas,"
URSULA K. LE GUIN

SLEEP

IF YOU EVER NEED TO—and I hope you never need to, but a person cannot be sure—if you ever need to sleep, if you are ever so tired that you feel nothing but the animal weight of your bones, and you're walking along a dark road with no one, and you're not sure how long you've been walking, and you keep looking down at your hands and not recognizing them, and you keep catching a reflection in darkened windows and not recognizing that reflection, and all you know is the desire to sleep, and all you have is no place to sleep, one thing you can do is look for a church.

What I know about churches is that they usually have many doors and often at least one of those doors, late at night, has been left unlocked. The reason churches have so many doors is that people tend to enter and leave churches in groups, in a hurry. It seems people have a lot of reasons for entering a church and perhaps even more reasons for leaving one, but the only reason I've gone to a church was to sleep. The reasons I've left a church were to avoid being caught sleeping or because I'd already been caught sleeping and was being asked to leave. Those are the only reasons I can remember, though I'm having trouble lately with remembering. I left some place, began walking, slept in all those churches, then everything else happened—that's all I know.

I don't think they're so great—churches. I don't think they're so great at all. That's not what I mean when I say you can go to one when you're tired. I'm not talking about grace or deliverance—a person cannot really speak of such things. What I mean is a church is a structure with walls and a roof and pretty windows that make it so you can't see outside. They're like casinos in that way, or shopping malls or those big drugstores with all the aisles, music piped in from somewhere, the endless search for that final thing.

But a church is also a building, often a sturdy building, and it can keep the outside far from you and when the outside is far enough from you, that is when a person can sleep. One thing it seems that every body needs is to sleep, and one thing people might not always have when they need it is a place to sleep or enough time to travel to a place where they can sleep, and so—a church. Maybe a church will fix this problem for you someday or maybe it already has.

For some time, I only slept in churches. A few nights I tried to sleep in some woods or a bathroom stall or behind a gas station, and I took a few good naps in a cemetery, but the only place I could ever sleep for any real time back then was a church. Since then I am not sure I've completely fallen asleep or woken up. Days and nights unspool together. Sometimes I think I might be writing a letter to sleep, that I might be asking him if he remembers me, if he ever plans on coming back. I've received no word from death's brother. I have not entered a church in some time.

The large churches, that's the sort of church you'll want to look for if you need to sleep. The large churches have more

4

doors that might be unlocked and more unlit spaces between all the buildings and rooms and hallways and playgrounds and gymnasiums and a kitchen or two and sometimes they even have a smaller chapel next to the larger one and the smaller chapel is almost always left unlocked. Also, the people that go to a large church are often too various to agree about anything in particular, so if you are caught sleeping there, the person catching you will likely not have a clear idea about how to proceed with getting rid of you (whether to call the police or the pastor, whether to give you something or take something from you) and people who are unsure of how to proceed are easy to escape. I have done this again and again. It seems that people who belong to a large church might want that church—so vast, so many rooms—to do the believing for them, but the church is just a building. The church has no thoughts. The church is brick and glass. If they ever slept there, they would see that.

I don't know how it all came to this.

It seems that time is somewhere else and what I can see here is not the present, but is, instead, the future, an eventual future, and somehow the present moment is back there somewhere I cannot reach and I'm stuck living here, in some future time. This body hangs beneath me, carries me around, but it does not seem to belong to me, and even if I could see them, I would not recognize my own eyes.

Now, never sleeping, I think often of the way life blinks at you when waking. I miss that kind of beginning, being given another day, taking another day, something that's yours, only yours, only yours and everyone else's.

If you do manage to have a night's sleep in a church, you'll notice how nice it is to wake up there. It will almost make you want to believe in God if you don't believe in God, and if you do believe in God, it will be a nice pat on the back for you. It must be so nice to be patted on the back in this way, to walk always followed by this constant, gentle pat.

IN A GAS STATION BATHROOM—piss on the floor, tampon machine, urinal, an open stall—I locked the door and stripped bare to throw water on my skin.

In a cracked mirror I saw these legs, saw these arms. I shut my eyes and tried to remember that body, but under shut lids the mind saw nothing, could not remember in what it was living. Again, I opened my eyes—saw this body. Maybe wider in some places, narrower in others, and some parts were soft, and some were firm, and where my legs met, there was something I knew to protect, though I could not say why.

When I put clothes on again, all memory of what this body was or is vanished beneath the cloth. It must be that I— whatever I am—am lying on the floor of a canoe, lying there, looking up at the sky. I am unable to sit up or move. I cannot remember getting into the canoe. Sometimes I hear people speaking to the canoe as if they are not aware that I am in here. Yes, that's what it feels like, what living feels like. Why is it so difficult to say as much? It never seems I can describe it clearly enough.

Once someone said I had a slender neck, a woman's neck, they said, a woman's neck growing from the thick shoulders of a man, but maybe it was the other way around—slender shoulders and a thick neck. Anything I remember being told about my body contradicts something else I've been told. I look at my skin and I cannot say what shade it is. I look into a mirror and see nothing in particular. It seems I am sitting somewhere within all this skin and muscle and bone and fat and hair. Can only other people tell you what your body is, or is there a way that you can know something truer about it from the inside, something that cannot be seen or explained? Over time, I know, bodies change—they expand and contract, skin turns papery or thick, new bodies grow within other bodies, limbs grow musky and must be cleaned, organs smuggle tumors through the dark—but isn't there something else? Something unseen. Why can't we ever speak to it?

In a gas station late at night the cashier gave me a biscuit and a wet hot dog. She showed me black-and-white photographs of herself from long ago—a young woman in high white boots, short hair round and firm and pure black. There in the gas station her hair had gone loose and gray. She did not ask me my name. She called me *baby*, called me *sugar*, gave me a sip of whiskey from her flask and let me sleep behind the counter. We were some distance from anything else, flat nothing around us, an unearthly glow rising from a town on the horizon. I slept on the floor while she sat up on a stool holding a newspaper in her lap, the other hand resting near a rifle. She was one of the few I've known who somehow knew to peer over the edge of this canoe and see me lying here—*hello*.

What are you? I was sometimes asked and I know it's rude to answer a question with a question but I have sometimes allowed myself to be rude in this way. I used to ask those askers, *What are you?* And what a horrible question to say or hear.

I regret ever asking it. Sometimes they answered me: *I'm a Christian, an American, I'm black, white, not from here, I'm hungry, I'm tired, angry, a woman, a man, a gay man, a pastor, Republican, mother, son, I'm forty-three years old, I'm homeless*, or sometimes they answered me with a laugh that rose and fell in their chests before it wandered away, leaving nothing behind.

When dawn came that morning in the gas station, the cashier gave me a carton of milk, said to come back if I ever needed. She never asked me what I was.

In the dark of the night with no one else around, she spoke to me—

I'm the only one who will work on Sunday. They all want to buy gas on Sunday, sure, but don't ask them to sell it. Strange thing is, people not working on Sunday is all that makes this place any good but it's also everything that's wrong with it.

She was quiet a long time, shaking her head, riffling through the newspaper.

Anyway the only good preacher I know isn't sitting up in any church just to get looked at. She's just the one that keeps the children all day, and sits in the hospice at night. She don't say nothing about God, the Bible. Don't have to. You see the way those children look at her—ask them what they know about. They know plenty.

SUNDAY

I woke up on a pew, sleeping on my side, knees bent. I did not move. I felt the warmth of another body near my head. I looked toward the floor, saw navy blue pant legs and two pale brown shoes. Above: the underside of a stubbly jaw. A large voice in the room like faraway thunder. My joints ached. I felt I'd been sleeping for weeks, heavy, immovable, mind empty, this body stiff against thin cushions.

Nearby was another person, in a blue dress that hung loose and long. Pale brown hair pulled into a knot at the neck. On the other side of this person were three children, boys, in little suits like the person sitting beside my head. The smallest was asleep. The largest was alert, staring forward, thick navy book in his hands. The middle-size boy was staring at me, and when our eyes met, he tugged on the dress. The person in the dress reached down and held that tiny hand still a moment, squeezed hard. The child grimaced. Hand released hand. A thought slowly came to me that this is the sort of person called a mother. A mother wears dresses, holds hands. Sometimes a word like this would appear, spoken by some silent voice.

Again the middle boy's eyes fell on me, his face more troubled this time, an angry, excited pain. The voice at the front of the room said some well-worn words and every voice in the room replied with their own well-worn words and the boy, still staring at me, murmured along.

The organ shouted a long chord, an opening, a call. The pews creaked as the bodies stood. The boy who had been staring at me grabbed the smallest, sleeping boy by the armpits and shoved him up to stand. Everyone sang in drone-y unison. Still, I did not move, stayed still on my side. The boy crawled down the pew toward me, pulled at my shoe until the mother reached back to smack the child's head. A mother smacks heads. A mother wears a pale blue dress and smacks heads.

Slowly, I stood to join them, was handed an open book, a hymnal. A finger pointed to a line of words, traced them along the page. I did not sing. Of most things I felt uncertain, but I was at least certain I would not sing.

Everyone sat again so I did as well. The larger bodies—the mother, the father (The father? The father)—did not look at me, acted as if I had always and would always be sitting and standing in this church, this pew. I was one of the things here: a hymnal, a Bible, an offering envelope, a tiny pencil. A person draped in heavy cloth stood at the front of the church and said things in such a way to make those words seem obvious and true, how simple the world was, how no one need worry about anything, how everything was here, all the answers were here and we could all just accept them, roll over and accept them like a sleeping body accepts air.

A gold plate was passed up and down the aisles, hand to hand to hand. People dropped in coins, bills, and envelopes, then passed the plates back to people who carried them to the altar like a casket toward its hole.

All the while an organ played. Someone stood near the organ, swaying and singing. Another someone carried a baby up to the altar and the person in the robes put water on the baby's head and the baby cried and the person in robes carried the baby around the room just as the money had been carried around the room.

The baby, wet and held out for all to see, wailed. The people in the pews smiled and the organ drowned out the baby's crying. An organ is a machine that can always cry louder than a human will.

At some point the father put a hand on my shoulder, looked down at me. The room of bodies stood again to sing, then sat again, listened to the person in robes speak, then stood to read words plainly from a page, then sat. Every time the bodies lowered themselves back into their pews there was a wooden ache, then a gust of silence.

Later, everyone left the church, flooding the aisles toward the church's many doors. I saw someone was carrying that wet baby, carrying it away, a limp human that belonged to whoever could carry it.

THE SIX OF US—the father, the mother, the boys, and I—
sat around a table draped with a white cloth. Plates of gra-
vied meat and bread and stewed-soft vegetables were passed
around, consumed in silence. People in white dresses carried
dishes to and from the tables. Across the room I saw one of
the people in the white dresses whisper to another, glancing
at me, then away. No one at the tables looked at the people
who brought the food to them, or if they did look, they looked
without looking.

I ate as quickly as I could, as much as I could. The smallest
boy stared at me while he was chewing. He opened his mouth,
showing me the mashed contents, sticking out his tongue.

Hilda and I have something we would like to say, the father
said.

Yes, Hilda said, putting her folded hands on the table. Hilda
looked at the father until he nodded his head. *Steven and I
decided that you can stay with us as long as it takes.*

As long as it takes, Steven said. *We'll move Jack down to the
boys' room and you can have the attic.*

As long as you need, Hilda said. Her attention was turned
inward and outward like a tightrope walker. I could hardly
look at her. Everyone at the table was looking at me except for
the smallest child, who stared at the ceiling, mesmerized, face

smeared with food. I looked at my hands, at the empty plate, at the soiled napkin in my lap.

And what do you think of that? Steven asked, his voice raised and hard, a ceiling.

I leaned back in the chair and nodded. It was all I could manage.

Steven and Hilda spoke to each other, to the boys. Several times Steven made long statements, then asked the boys, *Do you understand?* The boys replied by not replying but that seemed to be enough. When Steven eventually rose from his chair, the rest of them did the same. He joined a line of men beside a cash register and Hilda disappeared behind a pink door.

Boys, Steven said, *go on outside, go ahead and wait by the car and take our new friend with you. You're in charge, Jack. Be nice.*

Jack picked up the smallest boy and held him under an arm. The middle-size boy trailed behind them. I followed last. In the parking lot Jack dropped the smallest boy to the ground, then leaned against the family car, a big wide thing with huge wheels. The littlest boy moaned but stayed still at Jack's feet. Jack stared off, squinting, fists in pockets.

What is it? the middle boy asked, pointing at me.

He oughta be in the back in there, one of them that picks up the dishes, Jack said, spit shining a smashed bug from the car's windshield. *Everybody's got a place. Dad told me so.*

It ain't no boy, the middle boy said. *Ain't no boy I ever seen.*

Shut up, Jack said.

You shut up, then—she ain't even black neither. Don't know what she is, but—

Jack brought a hand down and threw his brother to the gravel.

You better—you better say you're sorry, the boy said from the ground. *You better tell Jesus or I'll tell him myself.*

It don't work like that, Jack said.

The boy stayed on the ground awhile, crying quietly and licking his skinned arms, catlike, attentive. He watched me as he did this, his eyes intent and still, as if this were a lesson he'd been taught and was now teaching me.

When Steven and Hilda came outside, Hilda took short, quick steps, her lips painted red, her cheeks pinker and eyes more pronounced. Nothing was on Steven's face. Nothing was on the boys' faces but dirt smeared with sweat. Steven opened the front passenger door for me. I got in. The boys packed themselves across the back seat. Just before we drove away, Hilda closed herself into the trunk.

THIS IS YOUR ROOM NOW, Hilda said as we stood still in the attic, the sloped ceiling nearly touching our heads. *I had Jack clear out some space for you.*

She pulled open a dresser drawer and left it open. I reached into my pockets and pulled out their contents—a nail clipper, dirty toothbrush, ballpoint pen, three coins, an oatmeal cookie wrapped in a napkin. I let all these things fall from my hands into the dresser.

The drawer was lined with old newspaper, the classified section, yellowed and falling apart in shards. One of the ads read—

> SON—You are not being
> hunted for anything but to
> find you. Come Home.
> —MOTHER

—and I wondered if this SON ever allowed himself to be found, if this particular SON had seen this paper and knew that he was the SON this MOTHER was trying to find, and I wondered if the MOTHER was really only hunting her SON for no reason other than to find him, if anyone could ever seek anyone for only one reason. It seemed she must have wanted something more than to just find him, and it seemed to me that a person might have many reasons, many many reasons, to not *Come Home*. But it only seemed that way to me and I am only one person, ruined by what I have and have not done.

Had there ever been a newspaper that would print the obituaries on the front page instead of the last?

The Reverend is going to come over for supper tonight, Hilda said. *He's concerned about you, of course, wants to make sure everything is OK. The whole congregation is concerned, but we know God sent you to us for a reason. He will take care of everything. It may sound silly in this day and age, but we still believe it. We can't help but believe it.*

Hilda looked out the window over my shoulder, looked to me again, away again. I felt this gentle urgency around her, a bruised kindness, as if something had been threatening to destroy her every day of her life and her only defense, somehow, was to remain so torn open. She kept shifting her weight from one leg to the other, looking at the floor. She told me she was someone that I could trust, that I could tell her what had happened and where I'd come from and whether I was a boy or a girl, and I could tell her how I'd gotten into the church and how it was I'd come to sleep there, and I could tell her everything— and even if I didn't want to say a word to anyone else, it was safe, she insisted, to tell her where my family lived or what had happened to my family if I had no more family—*even if they came here illegally*, she said, *even if they did something wrong, even if they did something not nice to you, or if someone else did something not nice to you*—and she took a long time to say all this to me, speaking slowly, pausing to give me a chance to reply, to begin—*it may not seem like it, but I really am someone you can talk to*—and even then it seemed to me she was a woman hanging off the edge of a cliff, telling me not to worry about her, asking what she could do for me.

But in her eyes—and not even so deeply—I could see she would not sleep so easily with a stranger in her attic, above her children. It's difficult to say exactly how I could see all this in Hilda's face. Perhaps an honest feeling will always find a way to force itself through, an objector crying out in a crowd, hoping someone will hear.

Do you understand what I am saying? Will you at least let me know that you understand these words, that you can speak English? She paused for a moment, then spoke louder and slower—*Do you speak English?*

I nodded, to which she nodded and smiled and said, *Dinner's at six*, then went quickly down the stairs.

All afternoon, alone in that attic, I listened to the noises that came through the floor—a rumbling of feet down a hall—a muffled conversation between Hilda and Steven—a door shut, a door slammed, a door opened and shut again. The caged parrot in their living room sometimes called out, *Hello? Hello? Hello?*—but no one ever answered. Silence for a while. *Hello?*

I sat on the floor, looking out a small window, staring down at the yard, feeling the sky slowly turn dim as Jack pushed a lawn mower in straight lines over the grass—across and turning and across again.

WHEN THE SUN STARTED GOING AWAY, I went down the attic stairs and stood in the hallway, hesitating in every direction. I could see Steven and Jack in the living room watching a television on mute, a football game. Steven explained each move to Jack, who nodded solemnly. The doorbell rang, casting a faint shadow over the room, though Steven and Jack sat comfortably in it.

Hilda ran past me carrying a wooden spoon and wearing an apron. The two smaller boys trailed behind her, pushing each other to try to take the lead. The doorbell rang again, then a knock, then the front door opened just before Hilda could reach it.

Hello, Reverend!

The boys latched on to the Reverend, one on his left leg and the other scaling his side.

Hello, Hilda! In the middle of cooking, I see?

And I'm probably burning something right now, so if you'll excuse me—Steven, the Reverend's here!

Hilda ran back toward the kitchen and Steven turned the television off, though Jack stayed still, stood only when his father punched his arm.

And our guest of honor, the Reverend said to me as he

stretched out both arms, half-laughing. *And how are we feeling now? Get some rest? Have a nice meal?*

I remembered his voice from the church, but now that he lacked a whole sanctuary between his face and mine, his voice was simple and fragile, like anyone's voice. I looked at the floor, at his feet in his shoes, thought of his toes in his shoes, here, standing in the living room like the rest of us. I looked up at his face, his neck. He stretched his arms out as if he wanted me to hug him or to allow myself to be hugged by him, to submit my body into his. I did not. He patted my shoulder, then left his hand there. He stared at me much longer and more carefully than anyone else had in a long time. I felt a kind of heat behind my eyes, a signal I couldn't decipher.

Now, what is it that we call you, dear? he asked. I looked at the empty television screen, saw ghostly reflections in it. *A name?* the Reverend asked again. *Really, whatever you'd like to be called, that's all we're asking.*

I didn't want to be called anything.

I thought of leaving the room. I thought of leaving the house and going somewhere, but I somehow couldn't. Some kind of force or threat was in the room, all over the house. The parrot called out, *Hello?* I gathered my hands in a fist behind my back.

Well, the Reverend said, *not much of a talker, now are we?*

All talk. No game, the parrot said. *All talk. No game.*

Steven and the Reverend laughed and the sons did not laugh. Jack muttered something under his breath, and Steven stamped on the boy's foot.

When my daughter was a little girl, the Reverend said, detaching one of the smaller sons from his body, *she found a stray kitten sleeping in a gutter near the church, and she just loved that cat and we still have that cat to this day and do you know what she decided to call it? She named him Gutter. How about that? Gutter!*

Hilda walked back into the room laughing and repeated the word—*Gutter! What a fine cat, that Gutter. How is he these days?*

Oh, he's doing fine, the Reverend said, *rather slow and fat but still the same ol' Gutter.*

Oh, how wonderful! Hilda said.

So if it's OK with you, the Reverend said, *how about we call you Pew for the time being?* He used that tilting tone meant for a question, but he wasn't asking me a question. *Until you get around to telling us something different? How about that?*

In the dining room Hilda ran from the kitchen to the table bringing out dish after dish, arranging them before us as we did nothing. Great heaps of fried animal parts. A bowl of potatoes, rolls, plates of meat and casseroles it seemed to take some strength to carry. Eventually Hilda sat beside me, smoothed her apron, and asked the Reverend to lead us in a prayer. Everyone had their eyes closed except for me and everyone had joined hands but I kept my hands joined to each other in my lap, so Steven put his free hand on the back of my chair and Hilda left her palm open on the table between our empty plates. The Reverend spoke a block of memorized text, nodding his head, agreeing with himself as he went.

And, Lord, help those having such trouble over in Almose-ville, help them see that all things are possible through you, and God bless our new friend Pew, Lord, a child of God just as we are

24

all your children, amen, and everyone else echoed the Reverend in that *amen,* all of them speaking together, even the smallest son.

Amen, the parrot said from the other room, though it seemed no one heard the parrot. *Amen amen amen.*

Well, the Reverend said, *ain't it nice to be here with a home-cooked meal?*

After everyone had eaten, the Reverend took me out to the front porch and we sat on a swinging bench he held still with his legs. He told me, quietly and not unkindly, that he really did need to know a few things about who I was, where I'd come from.

These are strange questions to have to ask, but we need to know them in order to provide you with a safe place to live. For one, and I'm sorry if this is embarrassing to be asked, but we will need to know if you're a boy or a girl. There's no reason for you to be embarrassed or ashamed or anything, and we don't think you've done anything wrong—we want you to know that. We really don't think you've done anything wrong, *exactly, at least not with regards to you not obviously being a boy or a girl the way everyone else is. What I mean is, you need not be ashamed of looking the way you do—as God loves all his children exactly the same—but it's simply not clear to us which one you are and you have to be one or the other, so unless you want us to figure it out the hard way, I think you should just tell us which one you are. Much easier.*

The insects sang in the heat around us. I looked back into the house through a window. Through two open doors I could see the edge of the parrot's cage, could watch the parrot side-stepping along its perch, bobbing its head, then stepping out of view, then into view again. I did not look at the Reverend. I had nothing to say.

Now, you might know that some people these days like to think a person gets to decide whether they are a boy or a girl, but we believe, our church believes, and Jesus believed that God *decides if you're a boy or a girl. So when you answer this question, that's the answer we want—did* God *make you a boy or a girl?*

I looked at the porch's ceiling, its floor.

It may be that you have some other feelings on the matter, that you're not really a boy or a girl, and that really is fine with us—we're very tolerant and you can think whatever you like, you really can—but just for our purposes, what is it that we would call you?

The Reverend was silent awhile, listening to the insects and nothing. For a moment the Reverend seemed to realize that his questions and statements kept leading us to the same empty place.

How about this—if you're a boy, if God made you a boy, clap once, and if God made you a girl, clap twice.

A mosquito was sucking blood from my wrist. I watched it swallowing and swallowing, then flying away. That blood was the bug's blood now, not mine, never mine again.

Whenever you're ready. Whenever you feel ready to clap, just go on and do it. Once for a boy and twice for a girl.

I thought of the message I'd seen in that yellowed newspaper—the mother hunting her son for nothing but to find him. I felt sure no one was hunting me for any reason, not even just to find me. I must have had a mother, but I also knew I didn't have a mother. I wasn't anyone's son or daughter. What a freedom that was and what a burden that was—to not have a home to go home to, and to not have a home to go home to. All I could have told the Reverend, if I could have spoken, was that I was human just as he was human, only missing a few things he seemed to think I needed—a past, a memory of my past, an origin—I had none of that. I felt I wasn't the only one, that there must have been others, that I was a part of a "we," only I didn't know where they were. We were and I was, not entirely alone. Maybe we were all looking for one another without knowing it.

I tried to remember at least one thing that had happened to get me here to this porch with this Reverend. I tried to go over it all, each event, to count the minutes out. The church I'd woken up in—that pew—the people who had brought me here—the meal and this. And before that? There was not enough time to remember it all. A moment only happens once but some of them take so much longer than a moment to understand, to see.

Well, if that's too much to ask right now, there are other things we need to know. How old you are, for instance, and we'll need to know where you came from . . . When were you born? And where? And what happened to your parents, your family? Did they . . . well. Are they somewhere else in the country? Or in another place? These are things we must know in order to give you the right sort of help.

The Reverend leaned back in the swing for a moment, then used his legs to rock it and us at the pace of a sleeping or dying heart.

I want to be your friend, you know. I want to be a good friend to you; I just need some help from you in order to be the best sort of friend I can be—do you understand? If you're already eighteen—if you're legally an adult, that is—then there are certain things we can do for you, but if you're not, then there are a different sort of things we can do for you. But first we need to know these things. Do you understand? These are just how the rules work. I didn't make them, but I do think it's best that we follow them, don't you? So that everything can be fair and orderly? You know, we treat everyone the same here—it's what we believe. Everyone gets the same kind of respect.

I stared out into the dark and still hot night and I listened to a thousand bugs singing the same note and I listened to the grass remaining still in the dark and humid air. There were many kinds of insects, I knew—I had seen many of them—but how many kinds of respect existed?

MONDAY

I WOKE UP still wearing my shoes and clothes, in the attic, on a bed, on my side, one foot already on the floor. Stray images passed through. A half memory of a place—a narrow hallway. I could almost see something else, could almost remember a word or sentence someone had said to me, but I could not tell if that had happened while I was awake or asleep. I could almost remember a feeling, an old feeling, the feeling of what it's like to be so small that anyone could just pick you up and take you somewhere. Once, I don't know when, I had been sitting in a diner and a small child was screaming and weeping and a person behind the counter was frowning at that child, telling the person with that child to make it stop, angry about being an audience to all that tiny pain. The person behind the counter must have forgotten the feeling of being so small that anyone could just pick you up and take you anywhere at any time. What a terror a body must live through. It's a wonder there are people at all.

HILDA TOLD ME that Steven had decided—and she agreed with him—that I could not be left in the house alone while everyone was at school and work and elsewhere, so she drove me down the block to a small white house surrounded by some flowering bushes, blooms all burst, the petals burnt brown.

Mrs. Gladstone will look after you this morning. Then someone else—his name is Roger and he'll come get you later. Roger is a very good friend of ours, so be good for Roger. He has something he wants to show you, or a sort of game the two of you can play together. Do you like games?

Hilda hesitated, briefly, waiting on some kind of answer.

Well, I bet you do. I think everyone likes games! Don't they now? Well—be good for Mrs. Gladstone—I know you will. She's very old and very tired. She's had a hard life and she just wants to be quiet . . . I'm sure you'll take to each other just fine. Hilda spoke quickly to me as we stood on the front porch, then opened the front door of this little house and shouted, *Pew is here now, Paulina—all right? Bye!*

Hilda shut the door and I listened to the fast steps taking her away from here. An old woman was sitting in a wheelchair in front of a blank television. The room was cold and punctured by a ticking clock. I sat on a couch covered in stiff plastic, wondering if anyone was ever intended to sit there. Maybe the couch was supposed to sit on the floor and be left alone.

It's only the fools you're fooling, Mrs. Gladstone said, speaking directly to the empty television. *Only the fools.*

We sat in silence for some time after that. It was not clear if she was talking to me. She could have been talking to herself or to someone I could not—for whatever reason—see. For a while there was this look on her face as if she were just about to say something or just about to sneeze.

I married late, Mrs. Gladstone eventually said. *I was already thirty-three if you can believe it, which may not seem so old now but back then it, well, I tell you, it was ancient. Everyone had given up on me ever finding someone and at that age no one has their pick anymore—even if you did once, you don't anymore. I can't be sure, since I don't know hardly anyone who is marrying age these days, but I think this is still true. A decent woman will take care of finding a good man quickly because it only gets harder and harder.*

But I suppose I was lucky, in a way. Charles, he was a widower and a good deal older than me, but that's what I mean about how you don't have your pick anymore. His first wife had been very beautiful, everyone agreed about that, but she had died anyway. Not from being beautiful, of course—I believe it was the cancer, though nobody said as much. That left Charles nearly fifty and with two children he didn't know much of anything about raising, so he had no choice but to go find another woman. Our mothers introduced us, then he decided it was best that we get married. And even though his children bothered me, I was more bothered by being so old and alone, so we did. It's a simple arrangement—marriage.

No one wants to say so, but it is. Maybe you'll see one day—when you're old.

A silence.

When you're old, Mrs. Gladstone repeated. *When you're old like me!*

She laughed a long time, or what felt like a long time. *Anyway—I was telling you about Charles. I keep getting side-tracked because I'm so old and useless—I forget everything. Everything.*

Charlie was beloved by the community—by everyone, every single one. And we were happy. He never even had to lay a hand on me, not even once, and there weren't many women in those days who could say that without blushing. Charlie and I had many good years together. No children of our own, though we did try. It's just that I was so old, and he'd already had two from his first wife, and they were a handful already. They were unhappy children, really just such a bother. I think he just didn't want all the trouble of having any more if they'd be like the first two. We traveled a good deal, up the East Coast, now and then to Virginia, and once to California. Once to Canada. He liked to drive and that suited me fine.

But then came the diagnosis and this was . . . well . . . almost twenty years ago now? Could it have been that long ago? We didn't have many options about what to do. Now it seems they have all sorts of treatments—but then, well, there just weren't so many. The doctors said he didn't have long, that we should get every-thing in order, to make arrangements and such. He talked to his lawyer about his last testament, I remember, and pretty soon word got around that he was dying, so the house filled with flowers and people—white people and black people and even that one Indian, or maybe they were a Mexican family, the one out on that county road that Charles had helped years ago with something—lots of people called on us, to him and me, bringing pies and such, and just so many flowers. So very many flowers. Then one night I was sitting up just looking at all those flowers in the front parlor, when the nurse came in and said to me—she said, I'm afraid this is it. He's going to God.

Mrs. Gladstone stopped here, her mouth hanging open, holding on to each word, blinking at them.

I can still see that nurse's face, and how she wasn't afraid of death, it being her profession and all, but of course I was afraid, just terrified. This whole life I had with him—just those ten short years after waiting for so long to have a husband, and now it was about to end and I really did believe it was God's will, but even so, that didn't seem to make it easy to accept. Maybe it should have, but it didn't. I knew I had to be strong and accept that God was taking him back now, but I have always had such a wicked heart—I just didn't want to be alone. I want to have my own way, always have been so selfish and wicked. I've deserved every bad thing that's ever happened to me, and I was so selfish that I hated God for it all—and I wanted to keep having a life with him. I loved him so much. I really did. He was such a good man.

She stopped again. Something in her face reminded me of a loose horse I'd found in some woods once, peace and terror tangled together.

I sat by his side, and his breathing went real slow and deep. The nurse left to give us privacy in those last moments, and just after she left the room Charles looked up at me and said, Darlin', *he said this all so slow and I remember his every word, he said,* Darlin'. Here I am. Just a man on my deathbed and now I must tell you that when I was a boy, such a long time ago, I was dared to hold a little black boy underwater in a creek down near the county line and I did it. Everyone said it was an accident, but it wasn't. It wasn't. I've thought about it every day of my life since then. *He spoke so very slow. He said,* I begged forgiveness from the Lord. I wasn't a very bright child—they even thought there was something really wrong with me—and it took me many years before I could think for myself, so when they dared me, I just went along with it. I went along with lots of things. We all go along with so much— you understand, don't you? *And then he said,* I repent, my Lord, *and I thought those were his last words*—my Lord. *I thought he was for certain going to die now. And I was so frightened by his confession, but I was also frightened to see him die, and I cried and prayed, but he didn't die, and all night he didn't die and we made it to the morning and he was still alive, just barely alive. The very next night the nurse told me that actually now he was dying this time, she was sure of it. And she did the same thing, left me in the room with him, gave us some privacy, and after some quiet hours Charles leaned to-ward me and said,* Paulina, dear, what I told you last night . . . *and I thought he was going to tell me it was somehow a lie, some kind of death dream, a hallucination of some sort, because how else could a person ever do such a thing? He was not a violent man, not at all, and I felt so sure it couldn't have been true. But then Charles said—*

Mrs. Gladstone stopped again. She was not crying. I don't know why I thought she would be.

36

He said to me, What I told you last night wasn't all of it. I was part of a group that hung those four men—do you remember? We thought one of them had raped someone's sister or someone's girl—I don't recall the details now—and we weren't sure which one. We hung all four. They were guilty of something, even though we didn't know what. We were angry, you have to understand. It wasn't easy, but we did it, about twenty or thirty of us. We had to. Even the sheriff was there. *And I did remember. It was four men from the other side of town, black men. There was a lot of disagreement between our side and their side. It was a painful time. A lot of folks moved away over it.*

That second night, he didn't say he repented or that he knew it was wrong . . . But again, he didn't die. He somehow lived to the next night, and he confessed to other things he did or secrets he kept for other men, worse things and things that didn't seem that bad, and I won't ever know if any of it was true, and there's a chance, maybe even a good chance, that all of it was some kind of brain problem that happens to people toward the end, you know. He watched a lot of movies, and he liked the violent ones—I don't know why.

But I still can't help but wonder if what he'd said had really happened, if he had been one sort of man when he was younger and another sort of man by the time I had met him. The man I knew, he was gentle and kind, kind to everyone, everyone, never had a sour word about anybody. Never even laid a hand on me. But if it was true—well, something of that first man must have remained in the man I knew, only I couldn't see it. And since then I keep thinking

37

about how you can't be sure of who someone really is, or really was, before you knew them . . . or even after, sometimes. I just—

She turned to look straight at me, and only then could I see that one of her eyes was glass, still and empty and shining. A little gold cross hung around her neck.

You know . . . What Hilda told me about you on the phone don't really line up with what I'm seeing here. She studied me for a moment, one eye intent on me and the other empty, peaceful. *I suppose it don't matter. It don't matter to me, not me, not one bit. At least I know a little about what it's like to stay silent. I don't know much, but I know at least that one thing.*

We sat quietly together for several minutes and listened to a grandfather clock ticking.

Charlie finally passed after about a week of almost getting there, then all the flowers in the house didn't smell quite so good. The house cleaner asked me if she could throw out the wilted ones but I told her to just leave them be. Some time later I took them out to the backyard myself, let them rot in a pile.

WHEN THE KNOCK CAME, Mrs. Gladstone looked at me then back to the empty television. I went to the door, opened it. Someone was there.

I'm Roger, the person said, offering me an open hand. *You must be . . . You must be who I'm here for. Mrs. Gladstone can get tired easily, so they told me to come get you—Steven and Hilda— they told me to come get you about now. I thought maybe we could take a walk before it gets too hot?*

Roger wore a short-sleeved white shirt and a thin black tie. He had a dog with him, pale fur, a dense animal that muscled along, kept his leash taut. We walked along a street shaded with heavy oak trees and large houses set back on wide green yards. Sprinklers spun water across the grass.

You know, it's odd for us to have a visitor. We don't get many visitors. People don't really pass through town so much. We don't even have an interstate.

I was watching our feet on the sidewalk—our pace had matched exactly, as if we were each walking beside a mirror.

When I was about your age, I guess, I started going to Quaker services. I lived up north at the time, in a big city, and the noise bothered me, the people bothered me, and I wanted to go be quiet, to go be with quiet people. I don't know if you know this, but the Quakers, in their services they don't have a preacher or anything because they believe that everyone should just sit in a room together and not say anything at all unless they're really moved to do so in that exact moment. So, I suppose this particular congregation was moved all the time—someone or another was constantly getting up to speak. Some days it felt like there was barely a minute of silence.

The dog with us began barking at another dog on a porch far behind a fence we passed. The other dog was yellow and lean, ill or asleep, his paws limp and hanging at the top of the porch's stairs. The yard in front of this house was mostly dead grass and rocks and a tricycle pushed over on its side.

Roscoe! the man said. *I don't know what's gotten into him. He's not usually like this.*

Roscoe went on barking and growling, but the yellow dog hardly lifted its head. Eventually Roscoe gave up and resumed walking.

He's not usually like this, Roger said again, shaking his head.

Anyway—the Quaker services. I remember sitting there one day and this young woman got up to speak and she was sitting at just the right angle to me that I could see that there were tears in her eyes and she looked sort of weak, like she was about to faint. And as she began to speak, I sensed the room was really listening to her, which was a little unusual—most people who spoke up did it too often, so no one ever really listened to anyone, but this woman—well, I felt I had never even seen her before, much less heard her speak. She seemed uncomfortable—and she took a while to start. I don't think I had ever felt as moved by just the sight of a person as I was moved by the sight of her—though I was quite young, maybe your age, I'm not sure. It's not that she was very beautiful or something—she was quite plain, if I remember correctly, but she had some kind of elegance—it's hard to explain. It seemed she'd been hurt very badly and was surviving it in a way I was only beginning to be able to recognize. When she finally did begin to speak, she did so very slowly, almost as if she'd practiced—which would have defeated the whole purpose of a Quaker service, if you ask me, you know, practicing at home so you can get it perfect—but anyway, I'm not saying she had rehearsed it or something, but there was something so complete and final in what she said. It was just—well, she was actually—she really had something to say. It was only a few sentences, but I remember how when she was done and had sat down again, I tried to force myself to remember exactly what she'd said. I kept repeating it in my head, because it had seemed so useful and true—so I was trying to hold on to those words, and I was repeating and repeating them, but already they were falling apart . . . I was already forgetting it.

Then a few minutes later, a man got up to speak, and as soon as he began, I forgot all of what the woman had said—even the most basic idea of it. And that's part of the problem with the Quakers, at least to me, because in the end no matter what a person says in that room, it will always be misunderstood, then forgotten.

Roger and I were quiet for a while after this. We kept walking. I could see that his white shirt had gone translucent with sweat at the armpits and the center of his back. The dog panted and occasionally growled at nothing in particular as he led us down the sidewalk, his feet moving quickly on and off the hot pavement. Sometimes I felt we were all breathing in unison, other times it seemed we had no relationship to one another, that he was walking and I was walking and neither of us was

41

even aware that the other was there, that even if I hadn't been there, he would have told this story to the dog or to the lawns or the trees or the air.

What I'm trying to say is that I understand why a person might want to be quiet for a while. And you don't have to say anything, if you're not ready. You don't have to say anything at all to me, if you don't want to.

We went on. I looked forward, down the long sidewalk. Somehow the streets had that feeling, that holiday feeling— and I wasn't sure how I knew this feeling but I did know it—a vague sense that everyone is gathered somewhere else and they don't plan to come out until it's over, until whatever it is that is happening is over. No cars were moving. No people walking. Only sprinklers spinning water in great, dissolving arcs and me and this dog and this person making our way through the heat, walking toward what I did not know.

But at some point you have to ask yourself, Roger said, *whether remaining silent is something that is having a positive effect or a negative one on your life. You have to ask yourself whether it's something you're doing or something that's being done to you, from the inside, from something else.*

We walked for a while longer. I stopped paying attention to the sidewalk or trees or heat. Eventually I heard Roger unlatch a gate. We went up a gray stone path to a gray stone house. The front door was unlocked. The air inside felt like that of a cave. Light blue walls and the furniture, too, was all upholstered in blue variations—navy sofa, teal rug, and water-colored curtains.

I've worked with cases like yours before, he said. *Or, well, not exactly like yours, but very similar. There's a family at the church who adopted a refugee child, an orphan from someplace having a war, and even though they had been told the kid was fluent in English, he had a pretty bad case of nerves when he arrived, wasn't speaking at all. Actually, I believe you're going to visit them, Hilda mentioned that they'll take you to dinner at their house tonight. Anyway, Nelson—that was the name they gave him for some reason—after I worked with Nelson for only a few weeks, he was fine. He had seen such terrible things, his whole family killed, his neighborhood bombed, but there's really nothing a person can't overcome, you know—and for me, I think that's because God really is looking out for each of us. I'm not saying you have to believe that if it's not right for you—I'm not that sort of Christian that thinks everyone has to believe the exact same things for this to work—but I do believe that I can use what I know and feel to help you.*

Roger pulled out a large binder and opened it on the table in between the chairs where we sat. It was full of simple drawings in plastic sleeves, all the lines unsteady. He flipped through a few of them before stopping at a page covered in thin lines. A small purple form was lying at the bottom of the drawing and above it were various human-looking shapes, red scrawl spewing from them. The forms were intricate but inexact—a hole not clearly an eye or a mouth, a long gray shape either a gun or sword.

This is one of Nelson's drawings of a dream he has had since he was very young. He kept having the dream after he moved here, but after we worked together for some months, he stopped having the dream.

Roger smiled and looked at the drawing awhile longer before closing the binder and putting it away.

You see, what sometimes happens is that a person is witness to terrible things or sometimes those terrible things happen directly to a person and even though that person will usually stop consciously thinking about those unhappy memories in order to move on and function in society, sometimes a part of a person's mind won't stop thinking about those terrible things until we find a way to express it, until we find a way to get it out of our head. For Nelson, expressing these things in words was just not possible, but drawing helped him stop thinking about the past and start thinking about the present. The family that took him in—I mean, his new family, his legal family—they have been very fortunate so they can provide everything that he needs. Nelson doesn't have to worry about anything, so he doesn't. It's very simple—you can't allow yourself to be troubled by trouble that's not there. Now Nelson is a very easygoing guy, and I'm proud of him, for overcoming everything. When you meet him, you'll see—he's still quiet, but he's calm. You'll see.

WE STOOD ON THE DOORSTEP of a house so large you couldn't even see much of it from the street—half of it hidden behind trees and sculpted hedges. Hilda rang a doorbell, and the more I thought about entering the house, the less it seemed possible that I could be let into such a house—that I was somehow not large enough to be inside this house, that it was simply not for me to know. Could someone call this a house? Could a person really walk up to this thing and believe it to be the person's home, larger than a school, larger than most churches?

A woman answered the door saying so much and so quickly—*Welcome, welcome, it's so good to see you, come on in, it's so nice to have everyone over like this! Come on in and get out of that heat.* Her hands moved around wildly, waving us in, grabbing the boys by the face and kissing them, wrapping her arms around Hilda and Steven and finally landing on me—

Aren't you just a doll? Aren't you though? Isn't this one just the sweetest, have you ever met a sweeter doll than this one? Have you?

No one answered her. The woman clutched me for a moment—*My name's Kim, but everyone calls me Kitty, so you can go ahead and call me Kitty*—then waved her hands around, conducting us down a wide hallway.

Everyone's in the den having cheese and crackers and I hope you're hungry because I told our girl we were having special company and she just about pulled out all the stops. I went back there to check on her this afternoon and she was making things I hadn't even imagined about! And listen, y'all, if you need the restroom, it is just down this hallway here, down there and over to the right—of course I'd give you the full tour but it would just about take all night, and anyway I don't think any of the kids made their beds and I guess they hardly ever do so I don't know why I ask! Why do I even ask!

She stopped and picked up a bowl of white flowers from their spot on a marble pedestal.

Holly Henry did all these florals and didn't she do so good? She is so gifted. I have her come out here for all the holidays and the Forgiveness Festival, parties, things like that—and isn't this one nice here? I don't even know where she gets magnolia this time of year, she must be flying it in from somewhere. China? Imagine that, flying in magnolias from China! But they do smell nice, don't they? I do wish the magnolias bloomed around the festival— wouldn't that be nice? Have a good smell of them, go on—

Kitty kept speaking as we walked down the hall, but I didn't understand what she said. I felt the ceiling was too high above us, so high it might not have been there if I tilted my head up to look, so I did not look. We all walked deeper into the house.

At the end of the hall was a room full of leather sofas and chairs, all of them pointed at a massive television on one wall, an altar. Several people were in the chairs and sofas, all of whom looked like variations of Kitty—pale hair, skin gleaming as if damp, clothing spotless and pressed—all in blues and greens and whites, coordinated like an army. They stared through the television. A person in a sparkling dress was singing into a microphone in one hand. Something cloying and pungent hung in the air—not flowers, something else, something closer to the smell of a baby's head.

OK, company's here, y'all turn that thing off, will you? There's some lemonade here and Cokes if you want them. I can't handle the caffeine this late, myself, but it's there if you want it. And fix yourself a little plate here, too, but don't spoil your supper because like I said our girl has been cooking near all the ever-living day, excuse my language.

No one moved. None of us and none of them.

OK, y'all, really, turn that thing off now, Kitty shouted while smiling at the people who looked like her. A large man reclining in a chair watching the television, chewing a cigar butt, aimed a remote at the screen, making the singer vanish into gray.

Does everybody remember everybody? Well, y'all know Butch, of course. The man with the cigar put up a hand almost like a salute, a gesture that Steven returned. *And these are my daughters, Annie, Rachel, and Jill, and my sons, Ronnie and Butch junior,* the woman said, speeding through the names as if it was something between a prayer and a chore. The daughters and sons were all dazed, distant. *And where is Nelson?*

He's still upstairs, one of the daughters said without looking up from the screen in her hands. She was the smallest in the room but she looked the most identical to the woman. She and Kitty were wearing the same dress and sweater and necklace. Both of them had hay-colored hair sculpted into stillness.

Nelson! the woman shouted up a stairwell. *Company's here, Nelson, come on down!*

And, little darlin', the woman said, *remind me of your name again, will you?*

Pew, Hilda said. *It's just a nickname. For now.*

Pew! You mean pew *like a church pew?*

Yes, Hilda said. *It's temporary. It's just—*

Isn't that something! Hilda, can I get you a glass of white wine? I've got a pinot grigio open and Butch can fix Steven up with a glass of Scotch, how about that? But don't you go telling Joe or Mary-Lee that you had any fun over here because we always hide the liquor when they come over—ha ha!

Just what the hell is wrong with those people? Butch said to Steven.

Butch! Kitty turned to him with a face suddenly still and hard. *What did I tell you?* And just as quickly her face softened and loosened and laughed. *Well! Well, let me see about that pinot!*

I went back down the hall to where the bathroom was, passing a room full of trophies in glass cases, a room lined with wine bottles, a bedroom that looked as if no one had ever slept in it, and a room that was just empty, just a big empty room. Eventually I found the bathroom, larger than a large car, all marble and chrome, everything perfectly clean. I washed my hands for a long time, and when I came back out to the hallway, a short woman in a white uniform was there, waiting. She took my arm and whispered, *Habla español?*

I just looked at her and did nothing and she nodded as if something obvious had flown between us and we both knew exactly what it meant.

Sea lo que sea, pase lo que pase, puedes contarme. Recuerda eso.

She started back down the hall, stopping a few steps away to turn to me again—*Recuerda eso*. I looked at her. She looked at me. She vanished around a corner.

When I returned to the main room, Kitty shouted, *Now there we are!*—and took me by the elbow toward someone who didn't look like the rest of them. He was wearing a baseball cap and blue jeans and a loose white shirt. In the shadow of his cap, I could see a thick scar that ran from his temple to his neck.

The woman spoke quickly, gesturing to the person in the baseball cap, to me, and back again. She did not seem to notice or care that neither of us was listening to her. She said the word *Nelson* as if it were something she had long wanted and worked hard to own.

Hello. My name is Nelson. Each word was an exertion, each word very clear.

And this is Pew, honey, like a church pew, isn't that special? Pew's not much of a talker but I'm sure you two will get along just perfectly. Now, honey, I think maybe you've forgotten to take your cap off, honey, you know we've talked about that before, haven't we? About what to do when we've got company?

Let that boy alone, he's got his reasons, Butch called from the other side of the room where he shook a glass full of wet ice. The woman in white who had spoken to me outside the bathroom appeared beside him, refilled Butch's glass from a small bottle, and vanished down a hallway.

Without removing his cap or letting on that he'd heard anything, Nelson went to the refrigerator and took out a red soda can, opened it, and left the room. Kitty said something quietly for the first time since we arrived, something to Hilda and Steven, who each nodded with impressed horror. The woman in the white uniform appeared beside Kitty and said, *Dinner ready*, in a tiny voice, and everyone moved down another hallway, past various rooms and closed doors, flower arrangements, and hundreds of framed photographs of Kitty and Butch and these other people. Then we reached a room with a long table, huge bowls and platters of food, even more various and plentiful than the night before. Nelson was sitting at one corner of the table and I was ushered over to sit beside him. Once everyone had sat down, they all joined hands, but the chair to my left was empty and Nelson didn't take my hand, just squinted at me with something like a smile. Everyone shut their eyes while Butch said a list of memorized words, and when he'd reached the list's end, he added, *And God bless Nelson and God bless Pew, amen*, his concentration clumsy and honest, like a child gluing two pieces of paper together.

The plate before me was filled with food, soft heaps leaking oil. I had known hunger so well and for so long that fullness had been difficult to recognize, but now, faced with all this, I could hardly eat. Since I had woken up on that pew, the meals had been endless and I wished I could have reached back and given one of them to those days of hunger in the past, or that I could have moved this plate to a place—there must have been such a place—where someone else was hungry. Nelson ate as if in a contest with someone, his throat a constant swallow. How was it I could have forgotten hunger, that feeling I knew so well? Nelson stabbed the whole chunk of black meat from my plate and ate it, not looking at me.

The rest of the table spoke in overlapping voices, passing

bowls and platters around. The woman in the white uniform went around refilling glasses with water or ice tea or wine.

Nelson, having cleared his plate and mine, pushed his chair from the table, stood up, and I followed him by instinct.

Don't y'all want some dessert? the woman at the head of the table called out to us.

No, ma'am, Nelson said. *No thank you.*

It's pecan pie. I didn't think I'd ever live to see the day—

No, ma'am, Nelson said again. *No thank you.*

He's taken to playing checkers on the back porch after supper, she explained to Hilda and Steven. *Ronnie used to play with him, but he got tired of it I guess, so wouldn't you know it, now poor Nelson just plays himself, just sits out there and plays checkers against himself, so I guess it's good he has company today. I just really don't know how he does it, with that heat, must be something about where he's from, you know, must remind him of where he came from*—and Nelson shut the back door to mute her.

At the far corner of the screened porch was a low table with a checkerboard on it. Beside it were a few cushions he'd taken from the chairs and we sat on them, on the floor. From under the table, Nelson pulled out a large plastic cup with a straw in it and took a long gulp, wincing, then passed it to me.

Whiskey, he said, *and a little Coke.*

I took a long sip, thought of the woman at the gas station from some time ago. Even the haziness was hazy. I took another sip and felt my shoulders fall, felt my body settle lower into the floor. I smiled at Nelson. He smiled back, took the cup, and drank from it again.

I don't really play checkers, he said quietly, barely moving his mouth, glancing back toward the door. *I have my cup back here. They leave me alone and I have my cup. Two more years, then I'm gone. I'll go somewhere, and I'll never come back.* He took another sip, then spread the black and the red pieces around on the board, the numb action of something he'd done hundreds of times. *Never*, he said. He turned one of the black pieces on its side and pushed it forward and backward like a wheel that couldn't go anywhere.

How old are you? He waited a long while for me to reply. I shook my head. *I won't tell them you said anything.*

I looked out at the yard; brick pathways lit by tiny lamps wound between fountains and planes of grass and flower beds resting for the night. In the far corner of the yard a massive tree was spotlit from below, casting agonized shadows.

I don't know.

He nodded. *Where did you come from?*

I shrugged.

They really found you in a church?

I was sleeping, I said.

Yeah, not much else you can do there but sleep. They take me every week. My whole family was killed in the name of God and now these people want me to sing a hymn like it was all some kind of misunderstanding. Must have been some other guy.

He used a red piece to jump diagonally over a black piece, then used that black piece to jump diagonally over the red, a game against himself.

I'm not as stupid as they think. I've read the history books, their Bible. It's all in there. He stopped the game abruptly, leaned back, his head seeming loose on his neck. *You're right not to say anything. They hear what they want. The more you say, the more they'll use it against you. Maybe they'd leave me alone more if they thought I was a mute.*

He took another sip, offered me another, and I took it. He put the cup back beneath the table just as we heard the door open and Butch calling out at us.

How y'all doing out there? A cigar mumbled his voice.

Good, Nelson said.

Who's winning?

Pew, Nelson said.

Very good. Butch shut the door.

Nelson leaned over his knees, an elbow on each, and looked at the floor awhile.

You're all right—I haven't met many people that were all right, not here, but . . . you're OK.

He kept looking at the floor, and when he spoke again, his voice went lower and looser, as if it were falling apart in water.

I'm just sorry you came here or got left here or whatever. And maybe when I'm eighteen, I can help you leave, too, but right now I have to go. I have to go do something, all right? And you should just stay here. Butch probably won't check on us for a least a few minutes. You don't have to go back inside or anything, but I'll meet you back here in ten minutes or something. OK?

I nodded.

You can have the rest of my cup, he said as he went out into the yard. I listened to his steps quicken through the garden until I couldn't hear them at all. The spotlighted tree was still out there, and without making a choice I was already walking out toward it, pulled by its wooden ache. Why couldn't they turn the lights out for him? Why couldn't they let him sleep in the dark? I stood in front of one of the spotlights on the ground and tried to cover it with my hands, but it was no use.

Nelson, is that—

Kitty was there, a cigarette in her hand.

Oh, little Pew darlin'. I thought you were Nelson. He's often running around out here at night. I usually don't—you know this stuff will kill you, it will, but it—well, it has some good qualities . . . does some other things before it does you in.

She laughed a little, a lonely laugh that ended quickly.

This time of year—it just makes me nervous, so I let myself have one in the morning and one after dinner just for the week before the festival. She was looking past me, back toward the house where the windows glowed yellow. *It's a good time of year, a beautiful time of year, but I don't know—it just makes me a little jittery.* Her eyes looked different out here. It seemed she couldn't bury herself in them quite as well.

She looked up at the tree and took a long drag. *Doesn't it look like it's about to grab something? I just love these oaks, live oaks I believe is what they call it. I wish I knew all the plant names out here, and I've tried, but I forget them all the time . . . I do know that's a dogwood over there.* She pointed with her cigarette, then took a long drag. *And that's a magnolia, both of them over there, magnolias, smaller ones.* The magnolia seemed somehow exhausted, weighted and weary under all those dark green leaves.

I do wish they bloomed this time of year. It would give me some relief. But you can tell a tree whatever you like—it won't ever listen!

54

We stood there quietly for a while, listening to her smoky breath and the faint crickets all around us.

Strange you showed up this week of all the times you could have. Now, I don't know what anyone has told you yet about this weekend, but it's nothing to worry about. I'm sure Nelson would be happy to share with you what he's learned about it—he really has come to enjoy the festival, I think, and things are much easier at school for him after it's over. You'll see. The time right after, everyone's more peaceful. Of course right now it's a little more dangerous for everyone . . . the week before especially. People get a little anxious I suppose. Start acting out. It's just human nature.

But it really does wonders for the community. I remember when we first started the festival, some years ago, and all the reverends at all the churches had to convince us it was a good thing to do, then the day after it was over I turned to Butch and said—Butch, for as much as people like to talk around here, there sure are a lot of things they don't say!

I watched the smoke fray in Kitty's laughter.

Kitty put her cigarette out on the ground, then stored it in a tiny glass jar she pulled from her purse. She looked up at me as she screwed the jar lid on tight—*You know I would just about die to have skin like yours—what is that, just genetics? Does it run in the family or something? Must be. It's like baby skin, but you aren't so young that you'd still have your baby skin.* We began walking back toward the house.

With us—well, our skin is just falling apart from day one! Ha ha! Just wrinkled and blotchy and terrible unless you spend a lot of money on it. Ha! Isn't it just so ugly, isn't it though? Skin—isn't it just terrible? It doesn't give you a minute of rest, does it? Not a single minute!

Nelson stood at the screened porch as we approached.

Look who I found in the garden, Kitty said to him.

Yep, Nelson said.

Were you showing your new friend around the garden? Isn't that nice?

Kitty took a mint from her purse and put it in her mouth, then sprayed perfume in her hair and across her dress. Butch was just inside the door as we all went back inside.

I wish you wouldn't spray all that junk on every night, Kitty. It don't cover nothing up anyway.

Just having a walk is all, Kitty said. *You know how I just love to see the garden at night. We were all out there walking together.*

TUESDAY

ROGER SET A STACK of white paper and a box of colored pencils on the table before me, but I only wanted to stare out the window over the sink, watch the way the wind moved the big, flat leaves on that tree out there. Roscoe slept beneath the table. Roger kept telling me he had all day, we had all day, that we could just sit here doing nothing and that would be fine. Sometimes he'd roll a pencil toward me and suggest I could draw what I was thinking, to just relax and think about where I'd come from, to relax and think about who I was and what had happened before I got here.

It doesn't have to be anything in particular. It can be abstract. Do you know what abstract *means? It means it doesn't look like anything real, just shapes that look like nothing, or maybe that look like a thought . . . or a feeling. Just shapes and colors, lines, whatever you like.*

Roger picked up a sheet of paper, took out a gray pencil, and drew a large square. He looked at the square for a moment, then drew another square inside the first one. He slid the gray pencil carefully back in the box, took out a red pencil, and drew a red line through the center of both of the squares.

This is a picture of how I feel right now. And this is abstract, though I guess you could say it looks like something, sort of. You could say it's a television screen or map or something, but it's really not anything in particular. That's what abstract *means. Just feel-ings. Do you understand?*

I nodded. Roger nodded. He looked down at his drawing, seemed to make some sort of decision about it, then put the page aside.

Would you like to have a try? Maybe you could draw some-thing about how you're feeling this morning or something you've felt in the past. Something about where you came from. Something you remember. It doesn't have to be perfect. And you can start over as many times as you like—rip them up, throw out anything that doesn't suit you. You can make as many drawings as you want.

I thought of that white heron I'd seen flying over the edge of a darkening row of trees, just after dusk, some night I couldn't find a church and ended up sleeping in a field. Two herons had been there, waiting for something it seemed—always it seemed as if a heron was waiting on something to happen. I watched them until it was too dark to see anything.

I took a pencil and drew the shape of a heron flying some distance away. The paper was white and the pencil was white, but the faint shape of the heron—its wings, neck, head, body— made a smooth, raised shape on the page. I took a gray pencil and a blue pencil and filled in the rest of the page around the heron, filled it slowly with thin, hatched lines, then slid it across the table to Roger.

Thank you, he said, studying the page.

He said other things, said them all so quietly, carefully, ex-plained something about the way that he *works* with his *clients*, what he does with the drawings, what they can tell him—*what they can tell us both.*

I listened but I did not listen. I avoided his eyes. Beneath the table the dog snored and sighed. Outside the branches on the tree had stopped moving, sat still as a photograph. Roger put more paper and pencils in front of me, asked me to draw what this drawing made me feel like. *It can be abstract*, he said. I felt some kind of sideways tilt in the middle of me.

Are you comfortable? And how are you feeling—are you feeling all right? Do you need any water, anything?

I shook my head.

All you need to do is try to remember what it was like to make this drawing. Can you do that for me? Just make a drawing about that drawing, a feeling about a memory. We're just trying to create an understanding—do you understand? That's what people do. We can't live each other's lives, and we can't see each other's memories or feelings, so we try to find ways to share them with each other. What is next to this memory for you? What are the other memories or feelings that sit close to it?

I thought of almost nothing. Roger watched me and made notes on a large yellow pad. I listened to the pencil whispering across the page. Roscoe was standing under the table, then jumped into my lap, and when Roger tried to pick the dog up, Roscoe just growled and snapped at him, then looked back up at me with still, watery eyes.

All right, Roscoe, have it your way, Roger said, but the dog did not respond to him in any way. Roscoe settled all his warm weight into my lap.

What has gotten into you? Roger asked the dog. The dog did not say. *At least he likes you. Some people—I don't know why— but he can't stand most people.*

I made no other drawings and had nothing else to say. Roscoe slept heavily in my lap and I watched the thick green leaves still or windblown all morning until Roger gave me a sandwich on a plate. Roger turned on the television in the corner with a remote and handed it to me. I put it down beside me and watched children eating bowls of cereal that made them grow wings and fly.

You can change the channel if you like. I'll be in the other room doing some work. Hilda will be over in a few minutes to get you.

When I looked at the television again, the children were gone and a man with gray hair and a suit was speaking about life insurance. I ate the sandwich. On the television was a map of the town with an animated curdle of clouds moving across it. A woman appeared on the screen, smiling, and explained what she believed the sky would do for the next five days.

I finished the sandwich. A metallic, meaty aftertaste hung around in my mouth. Roscoe licked my hands, stopping to bark at the sound of the back door opening, but quickly returned to his task. We heard Hilda's voice, a shutting door. Roger offered her a coffee. She declined.

Did it go all right? she asked.

Well, he drew something.

He?

Well—I don't know, really—

Their voices lowered, nearly vanished. Roger shut the door between that room and this one. The woman with the map was gone, and for a while nothing at all happened on the television. The screen went completely white and still and a smooth, clear silence took over until two men appeared, just as suddenly.

Beside them a little girl held a child-size guitar, plucking at it thoughtfully, seeming disinterested in speaking or being spoken to. One of the men said, *Play us a little song now, won't you?* She began to strum the guitar, quickly and intently, as if she were a little machine that had just been plugged in, her expression unchanging and sad. The adults clapped along; the girl played her fast music and the camera focused closely on the child's unmoving face, then cut to her quickly moving hands. Below it, a caption: CHILD PRODIGY STUNS LOCAL MUSIC TEACHER.

Roger has arranged for you to meet with someone out at Monroe Medical Center tomorrow morning, Hilda said after a minute of silence in the car. *He's concerned about what you've been through, and he wants to have a second professional assessment*. She was quiet again, saying nothing as we drove past several blocks.

I think it's a good idea, too. A second opinion. People always say that's a good thing. And they can do an examination out there . . . just a simple checkup really. Just to make sure everything is OK. Anyway, right now we're going to see the children's minister. He asked for a visit. Sonny. Everyone calls him by his first name like that. He's very casual. He runs the youth group and some other things.

When we got out of the car, I recognized the church where I'd been found and for a moment I wondered if they had decided to put me back in that pew, let me disappear into wherever I'd come from. I followed Hilda through a side door and down a hall covered in thick red carpet. I followed her up a wide staircase and down another hall to a black door on which the words THE CHILDREN'S MINISTER were painted clearly in white. Through the floor I could hear a piano starting and stopping and beginning again, someone practicing chords. Hilda knocked on the door and someone shouted, *Come in.*

64

The room was filled with plants, green vines climbing and hanging around a window. In several places around the room there were little bowls of small purple candies. Sonny came toward us, spoke some words, took one of Hilda's hands with both his hands, and shook vigorously. Hilda turned to me and said, *This is Sonny*, then turned to Sonny and said, *This is Pew*.

Sonny smiled.

Well? Hilda asked all of us and no one at once. *Suppose I'll leave you to it*, she said, and was gone.

Sonny looked as if he'd just been given some terrible news and was trying to keep it a secret. He took a small handful of candies from a bowl on his desk and pushed them into his mouth while he gestured to me to sit in a plush armchair on one side of the room. He took a seat in one across from it and pushed the bowl of candies toward me.

It's my weakness. What a sugar tooth I've got.

He put another handful in his mouth. The little table between the two chairs held a potted flower, a deck of playing cards, and three thick books, their spines unbent.

You've made quite the stir in town, as I'm sure you know. It's not often we get visitors. Tourism isn't exactly a business here. He smiled, bent one leg over the other. Below us I could hear the piano starting up again, voices collecting in a room— something sounding almost like rain on a roof—someone laughing, someone else laughing, then everything stopped and one voice was speaking, then singing with a few simple piano chords.

Choir practice, Sonny said. *Tuesdays are my favorite. Did you hear them last Sunday? Well, sure you did. Just beautiful.* The piano began louder this time and a group of voices began singing in unison. Sonny was listening, his eyes lowered and his ear angled toward the floor. He made silent words with his mouth.

Oh, how great they're practicing this one today . . . He leaned back in his chair. *How perfect.* The voices became clearer and Sonny sang along with them.

He hummed and mumbled along with the piano's chords. *I don't know the verses by heart. Was never so good with memorizing. But I do remember the story about this one, I think. Was written by some guy in the nineteenth century, I think it was, can't remember who, but he was a composer, a songwriter, wrote hymns, maybe other songs, too, and one day he gets the news that his four daughters—I mean, four daughters! Could you even imagine—anyway he gets the news that the ship his daughters were taking across to America from England, I think—anyway he gets the news that it wrecked and they're all dead. I think maybe his wife, too, or maybe she had just died before this and maybe he had one son—I feel like the son was dead, too, but for sure the four daughters all died in a shipwreck and he gets the news and sits down and writes this song— "It Is Well with My Soul." It's just all about how no matter how hard things get, no matter if Satan tests you or everyone you love dies or something else, you just have to keep your head up, you have to keep your eyes on the Lord. That's what I take it to mean anyway. It's real easy to feel sorry for yourself when bad stuff happens, even really bad stuff. But you can't—you just can't. You don't even have to think about it. Of course, it's not easy to do this, you know. It takes practice, and it doesn't always come natural, you know, at least not for most of us.*

Sonny nodded to himself for a while, listened as the choir below us sang those lines again. *It is well*, they sang softly, *It is well*. The piano stopped. Someone was talking. Sonny took another purple handful from the bowl. The piano began again. *It is well*, they sang, louder, then again even louder. *It is well, it is well . . . with . . . my soul!*

I hear you met Nelson? Sonny asked.

I nodded. Sonny threw the candies into his mouth and began talking through them.

What a guy, right? And he has seen a lot. He's a lot like you, in that he doesn't like to talk about it, but man oh man. Sonny looked out the window, quietly chewing and swallowing, his eyes scattered, his head shaking. *He saw his whole family get killed, nearly got killed himself, then he had to go through all this difficulty with immigration—I can't even tell you how complicated, just ridiculous, inhumane—even though there was already a family here ready to take him in and everything. He didn't even get here until almost two years after he was supposed to. Had to live alone in a refugee camp, thinking he might never get out. Barely any school, barely anything at all. Now, of course, he's got a good life, nice house, a family that can take care of him, the whole world opening up—but, man, he sure had to suffer.*

Sonny looked out the window again, put his hand to his brow as if trying to shield himself from something. *You know, everyone is wondering what you've been through. It's not really anyone's business, you know—and we know that. A person's life really is just between them and the Lord and their family, but we do wonder what we can do to help. And we'd know how to help better if we knew a thing or two about where you came from.*

Sonny shuffled a deck of cards and started to deal out a game of solitaire. I remembered watching that old woman at the gas station playing it, explaining it to me—*It's a game for people who don't really like other people*, she said.

It's a confusing time, isn't it? Sonny asked me. His teeth, when I saw them, were faintly lilac. *Countries, governments, are killing people in heaps, tearing cities apart with war, killing women and children.* He was playing his game rapidly, turning over this card and that, dwindling the deck, which was soft and worn at the edges. *It's a horrible mess, you know. Everywhere you turn, people are hurt. It even feels some days like men and women right here in our country have turned against each other. All this bitterness. Everyone wants to be the one who's right.*

He laid one card down slowly and firmly, then smiled some private smile.

Life is suffering—it really is. The Buddhists are right about that one, I tell you. Nothing is easy on this earth. Even that hymn I was just telling you about—well, only a few months after that guy finished the lyrics, the guy who'd written the music to go along with it was on a train and it fell off the rails and he died, too. So this one man loses his whole family, then loses the guy who helped him write the song about losing his whole family.

Sonny's game of solitaire was already over. He had won, I suppose, so he shuffled the cards into a single stack again and took another handful of the candies.

*What I am trying to say—and I'm not like the Reverend, not as good with the big speeches, you know, on the spot—*and Sonny paused for a moment, his whole mouth a darker purple now, tongue and teeth unreal and inky. *What I'm trying to say is that* *no matter what you've been through, there is a place here for you. I don't think it was an accident you chose our church to sleep in, that we found you here. And when you're ready to talk, kid, I am here to listen.* We stood and he held my shoulder and looked down at me. Below us the choir was still singing. Their voices shook the floor.

FINE, HOW ARE YOU? the parrot said, facing a wall and nodding its head. *Fine, how are you?*

I sat in the little room just beside the kitchen, with a glass of cold milk, and *something sweet*, Hilda said, a square of black cake, to end the long day I'd had. I stared out the windows at the night sky, and when I reached out to touch the glass, it was still warm. The heat had not left, never left, was constant.

Through a wall I could hear the murmur of the television that Jack was watching, heard the thump of a ball he was throwing and catching.

Jack, Steven shouted from the kitchen.

Yeah?

Turn off the TV and go to bed.

But they're about to show the replays—

Go to bed, Jack.

But Pew is still up.

It don't make a difference—Pew is not my child. I am telling you to turn that thing off and go to bed.

The television stopped. Jack stomped down the hall and slammed a door. The air in the house was still and smooth, broken only by Steven and Hilda's low whispers in the kitchen.

I shut my eyes and imagined a life in which only our thoughts and intentions could be seen, where our bodies were not flesh but something else, something that was more than all this skin, this weight. For a few moments I forgot where I was. I finished the glass of milk without realizing it, lost in the idea of a disembodied world, one where ideas could hold other ideas, where thoughts could see other thoughts and death couldn't end thoughts, where one remained alive by thinking and was not alive if not thinking. Somehow our bodies wouldn't hold us back the way they do here. Somehow our bodies wouldn't determine our lives, the lives of others, the ways in which one life could or could not meet the life of another. We would not have to sleep or slam doors or exist in these cells that eat other cells and die anyway, these cells we live in.

Fine, the parrot said, drawing the word out this time, then pausing a long while—

Fine, how are you?

Hilda and Steven came in, looking reddened and wrung out.

I reckon you won't start now, Steven said, *but if there's anything you need to tell us, anything you might need to come clean about . . . maybe you could tell us right now?*

Hilda reached over to take the empty glass and plate from the table.

Tomorrow will be even busier than today was, she said in a rush, *and you'll have to see this specialist way out in Monroe, the one that Roger arranged for, and the whole thing might be easier if you could speak with us a little before then. They'll need to do an examination. Just to make sure everything is OK.* I could say nothing. I could tell them nothing. We all sat quietly.

This Saturday, you may have heard, is the festival. It's a very important time of year and it's very important to us that everyone in town participates and understands how important their participation is.

It's really very beautiful, Hilda said, her voice spilling and loose, *very meaningful—*

Yes, and we expect that you'll participate with the rest of us, even if you might not fully understand what it means. Hilda had begun to cry a little. She wiped lightly at one eye, then the other, the first again, and on like that. Steven wrapped a hand around one of her wrists, which seemed to end something in her.

People will be curious about having a new person in the community, Steven continued. *It's only natural. So we just need to make sure that all is well with you, and you're suited to join us in this important event that we know outsiders don't always understand.*

We were all quiet for a moment. Some appliance in the kitchen grumbled.

Oh, Hilda said, *there is one more thing. I just thought you might be more comfortable if you had a bath. You hadn't had one since you got here, and I thought, well, you might like to have one. I've got one running in the washroom at the bottom of the stairs.*

We all stood and walked toward the washroom and Hilda went in to turn off the tap in the nearly full tub.

And if you'd like, Steven said, *Hilda could wash your clothes for you.*

I shook my head.

Are you sure now? Hilda asked. *It's no trouble.*

It's no trouble at all. She'll have them all pressed and ready for you in the morning.

I don't ever sleep, Hilda added.

She doesn't—she doesn't sleep hardly at all, not with all the laundry there is to do.

That's right.

Again I shook my head. They left me with the bath and shut the door. I took off my clothes. Steam wafted from the water and the water moved below, exerting the steam. I looked over at the water, then down at this body. Did everyone feel this vacillating, animal loneliness after removing clothes? How could I still be in this thing, answering to its endless needs and betrayals? The room was all white and gray and the air was warm and the air hung on me and I hung in this flesh that all those unknown centuries of blood that had brought into being. I had to tend to this flesh as if it were an honest gift, as if it had all been worth it. Why did living feel so invisibly brief and unbearably long at once?

I eased into the hot water and sat there for some time—seconds, minutes, I didn't know—then got out again, dried myself with a thick towel, put my trousers and shirt on, and went back into the hall. Hilda and Steven were still there, still in the dark, leaning together as if they'd just been whispering.

Good night, they said, first one of them, then the other. I nodded as I held one hand out to trace the hallway wall, making my way back up to the attic.

In the attic I lay down and could see the moon through that round window, full and pure white, so bright it almost seemed to be making a sound. Even through shut eyelids I could feel the moon's glare, so I lay there in that light, coming near something like but not entirely sleep, a stream of images or feelings going by, telling me nothing.

I was buried by night. The body is already dead, I thought. I was still smiling. The body is your tomb.

After some time, I got up, went down the stairs lightly so I didn't wake anyone, went through the blue-black house and out into the yard to see the moon more clearly. How lucky we are to have the moon. It seemed that hardly anyone ever saw the sky anymore. Had we all forgotten it was there? All this time below it, we forget. Maybe the sky will leave us someday, then we will be able to realize what it was.

I heard a door slam at the house and Jack came out. The air between us like a pool of warm water. Hesitating on the porch, he looked up at the moon, then at me. I half-sensed he wanted to frighten me, but I was not afraid—after all the moon was here, calm night, warm and easy air, and all of it was ours.

From the porch stairs he began to somehow yell and whisper at once—*We don't even know if you're a girl or a boy or where you came from or nothing and you're sleeping in my bed. In my bed. It's disgusting. You ought to go back to wherever you came from, go back there and leave us alone.*

Across the street a trash can was knocked over and a light outside a house turned on and a dog went running into the street, barking, chasing something. Then a car alarm went off, another car alarm began, and a cat hissed, screamed.

Jack kept walking toward me, still speaking in that yell-whisper. I moved out farther into the yard and saw an old woman standing in the window of the house next door, gripping her housecoat at the neck. I didn't know what to do with my hands, my body and I didn't know where it was allowed to go if there was anywhere I could go and not be seen, and when I looked back at him, Jack was facing the porch again, his father there now, saying a few firm, low words the way owners call back their dogs. Jack retreated, disappeared inside the house. Steven stood there in the porch light, staring at me for a while before I, too, went back inside.

Stay in your room, he said.

Halfway up the attic stairs I heard the door shut and lock.

WEDNESDAY

HILDA WAS DRIVING, her hair held up in curlers. We passed a green street sign—Stark Street. Maybe there was nothing else to say of that street. The sky was fading into a gray-blue. The moon hung like a ghost in the sky. I watched the light posts flick past the window, cows in wet grass.

I can't imagine what you've been through, Hilda said. Thin yellow light was beginning to flood into the car. *I think about it . . . I think about how easy my childhood was, and now my whole life is still right here in my hometown—the boys, Steven. My mother passed away when I was little, but I was never lacking a family. I had my father, my brother. And Mrs. Gladstone, the one you met the other day, she was my stepmother. Still is, I guess, and even though she never really got along with me, at least she never hated me, not completely, but anyway, I know everyone in town. Same church all my life. Everyone there knows me and I don't have to explain anything. Even had the same hairdresser for just about as long as I've had hair. This place, I know it's not much, but it's not really what some people think it is. It hurts me that everyone gets the wrong idea about it all the time, it really does.*

Though Hilda's face was completely still, she had begun to cry. She dabbed carefully around her eyes.

I'm sorry. I'm so sorry. I can get so carried away. I can get so emotional. Even a good commercial for something like the army or life insurance—they always get me. She was almost laughing at herself. *But I am very concerned about you. Everyone is. We just don't know what to do. We're just not sure.*

All feeling left her face, like that final shift at the end of a sunrise. She sat up straighter, exhaled, cleared her throat. She pushed the wadded tissues between the seat cushions. A firm daylight came down. The highway stretched ahead. Hilda pulled out a little bag and unzipped it while steering the wheel with her knee. She opened a tiny jar and spread something around her eyes, then ran a tiny black comb through her eyelashes, blinking.

I'm not used to an audience, you know. You probably think this is silly. I usually get all this done in the morning but there just wasn't time.

She ran a blood-colored lipstick over her mouth, then pressed her lips together. She put everything back in the bag, closed it, and tossed it into the back seat as if she wanted to forget the whole thing.

Paulina always said you had to make sure you were put together before getting into the car because if you're in a wreck and have to get picked up by an ambulance, you don't want to be looking a mess on top of all the rest of your trouble. Hilda laughed. *Oh, probably everyone's mother says that.*

We pulled into a parking lot beside a huge gray building.

I just have to deal with these, she said, as she started taking her curlers out. I stared the other way. It somehow seemed wrong to watch. Someone in a pale green uniform was pushing a person in a wheelchair up a sidewalk. A row of ambulances were parked next to us, waiting.

As we walked toward the hospital, Hilda's shoes clicked on the pavement, and though I had seen her only minutes before crying in the firm morning light, it now seemed she had never cried in her life, couldn't cry if she tried.

YOU WAIT HERE, Hilda said, as I sat. *I've just got a few papers to fill out before you can see the doctors—are you all right by yourself here?*

I looked around. She nodded and went away.

There were seven televisions around me, all of them playing the same station. A crowd of people had gathered somewhere with signs that said ANSWERS, NOW! and BRING THEM BACK. A man in a suit held a microphone to the mouth of a woman, who spoke loudly into it—

We have reason to believe that the town council or someone in the government knows what happened to the missing. That's what we believe, and we know we are right about what we believe. We're asking for them to tell us what they know, and—to at least tell the victims' . . . the families of the missing—

The woman's shouting voice softened and her face fell apart and for a moment she no longer looked like a statue of someone screaming, but something more like a pile of papers left out in the rain. She regained herself and continued—*My son, Vernon, he's been gone two weeks, and it's true some people here in Almose County underestimated Vernon, but I know he's a good young man and there's just no way he could just run off for no reason. I want answers. We all want answers—*

The screen cut to a reporter interviewing a child holding a picket sign:

NO JESUS NO JUSTICE
KNOW JESUS KNOW JUSTICE

The child smiled and spoke softly into the microphone held at her face, one hand waving her wide skirt from side to side. I did not watch the television after that, though I felt all the televisions were watching me.

Nearby there was a man with hair and skin the color of a dead sky, his stomach and chest rounded out, like a whole small person sitting on his own lap. Beside him there was an older woman wearing an apron, her dark hair pulled under a small white cap. In her eyes I could see an intricate calculation was always passing through her mind.

Sad thing with those people in the television, the man said.

Yes, sad, she said.

It's troubling to see. Very sad.

Hmm. Painful.

But they don't have to be in pain and they don't know it!

No, sir.

I figure we're lucky to be here where we are. We may have other problems, sure, but nobody goes disappearing.

Yes, a nice place.

No one would leave here, no one would just leave.

I don't figure so.

She cleared her throat very quietly and crossed her ankles. *Indeed.*

83

We're not perfect, of course. No one is.

Yes.

We know we haven't always been fair to everyone.

Certainly—no.

But we've always been fair to people according to what the definition of fair was at the time.

The woman nodded and fell within herself. It was somehow clear she and this man went along beside each other.

We've reckoned with it, he said, *and I, for one, I believe we are doing good.*

Good as we can be.

And ain't that enough?

Ain't it?

Yes, I'm so glad to be here, aren't you?

Aren't I?

Yes, aren't you though?

She removed the wax paper from a small sandwich and held it to his mouth. His feet and hands, I now saw, were held down by leather straps to the wheelchair he was sitting in. He bit into the sandwich as if to kill it, then bit again and caught the woman's finger. She yelped a little, dropped the sandwich into his lap, then picked it up and kept feeding him.

Beside me, a man with little wisps of white hair clinging to his head raised his cane to point at a television. On the screen a man was standing behind a podium now, his eyes calm and distant. Below the man a script—

> *Almose County Mayor responds to "Anti-*
> *disappearance rally."*

84

The man beside me shook his head, bore his hazy eyes into mine—

If you ask me, they shouldn't ever put a picture of one of these durn politicians on the television. We shouldn't know they durn names or they faces.

He sounded both angry and happy, pleased with himself and displeased with the world.

It's what makes the whole thing a mess—they ain't supposed to be looked at—they supposed to work. Same people that want the power want the fame, too, but I say we should never know them by sight or name—don't you think that'd work out better? We should just know what they can do and what they've ever done for other people and what they believe, what they think of things.

The man laughed into a cough. His face was falling off his head in a nice way, like an old tree. *But ain't that the problem? They don't think of nothing and they don't do nothing. They just want everyone to know they's in charge, that's all. We shouldn't be seeing any of their durn faces. They just want to be looked at. Can't hardly tolerate it.*

There was a cord running from the old man's arm to a bag of clear liquid hanging on a metal stand next to him.

Keep to yourself, don't you, kid? Always been just the opposite myself. Can't keep my durn mouth shut and looks like I never will.

It is strange how two lives can work themselves up to such a moment, idle in a waiting room, just to let something invisible pass between the two.

I reckon you've got it right, the old man said, leaning back, resting his cane across his lap. *I don't know anything, really, never have, never will. Should have kept my mouth shut, at least half the time.* He shut his eyes, seemed to fall instantly to sleep.

The television was playing a cartoon now. Something bonked something else on the head, and the bonked thing chased after the thing that had done the bonking, returning the bonk, turning to run away. The people in the room all watched it with some seriousness, even a kind of tenderness, as if they were looking delicately into the face of another.

I faintly felt an urge to speak, though I had nothing to say. I had nearly forgotten how to hold my own voice in my mouth. Someone in pale green pants and a loose shirt came up to the old man, leaned down to shout in his face.

Mr. Gladstone, we are going to have to take you back to your room again for your nap.

Without opening his eyes, Mr. Gladstone said, *I'd just as soon stay where I am. I've got this new friend here. Don't I now?*

Well, have it your way then, the person said, and left us.

Mr. Gladstone shifted in his wheelchair, trying and failing to find a comfortable spot. His eyes were still shut.

Some days I'd like to bust out of here, but I tell you, I wouldn't even know what to do if I did. Here, I get pushed around, they feed me this crap food—but out there, what? Nobody to push me around, nothing to be fed. I got nothing out there, nothing in here either. I reckon I'm here to the end. What a place.

I heard Hilda's shoes clicking toward us, slowing as she came near. She took a seat across from Mr. Gladstone, who finally opened his eyes.

86

My beautiful daughter, he said as he held a shaking little hand up, reaching and failing to reach her.

They let you sit out here? Hilda asked.

They still let me do a thing or two, he said. *Hadn't killed me off just yet.*

Hilda looked at him as if he were some impossible chore, then looked away. *So you've met Pew.*

Not much of a talker, Mr. Gladstone said.

I'm sure that suits you just fine, Hilda said.

We sat quietly a while after that, waiting. On the television someone was mowing a lawn. Eventually someone came over and wheeled Mr. Gladstone away without comment.

Bye-bye, he said, to which Hilda said nothing.

A nurse appeared—*The doctor's ready to see her if—oh, um, him?—I'm sorry, well . . . on the form it's not filled out—but, anyway, the doctor is ready.*

Hilda said something to the nurse in that soft, lost way of someone who had just woken up, though she had been sitting with her eyes still and open.

I'll be out here when it's over, Hilda said to me. *Be good.*

I'm Nancy, the nurse said as we walked, *and you can call me Nancy, how about that?*

We rounded a corner and went into a small room with a little padded table and two rolling chairs and a metal scale. I sat in one of the rolling chairs while Nancy lingered a moment in the doorframe, that little pinch in the face of someone trying to remember something. After a moment she said the doctor would be in soon, to just get comfortable for now and not to worry, that everything was going to be fine. Something in my face must have told her I didn't think anything was fine. She shut the door. Her footsteps retreated down the hall.

I sat still for a while, then the door opened. A man stood there still for a moment, already examining me, his face blank and hanging.

I'm Dr. Winslow—he put a hand out to me—*but you can call me Buddy, everyone calls me Buddy.*

I left Dr. Winslow's hand alone. He shut the door, lowered himself into the other chair.

First I would just like to tell you a few things about myself, about the work I do here, about the sorts of things I can do for you. My name's Buddy, as I said, and I'm a physician here at the Monroe Medical and Rehabilitation Center and I specialize, in part, in dealing with victims of trauma. Mostly soldiers, battered women, mental disturbance, that kind of thing. Sort of like our friend Roger, though his focus is children, I suppose, and Roger is really—how do I say this? . . . Well, he's had a lot less training than I have. I went to medical school, then did a residency up North, then I went back to school for several years, to a medical school that is just for people who study the brain. My degrees are there, you can see them.

He gestured to the other corner of the room where framed certificates hung useless on the wall.

Yes, you can see them for yourself, but what I am saying is, I have spent my whole life studying the brain, the human brain that is, and what happens to it over time and what happens to it when it goes through terrible things. Now, maybe you can give me a sign if I'm right, but I get the sense that you've been through something very difficult, am I right?

He stared at me.

Am I right now? Just give me a little nod if I am . . . He waited a moment, then exhaled, leaned back in his creaking chair.

We don't need to be this difficult, now do we? I even came in an hour early today, just to see you. So I would appreciate if you could also extend some kindness and understanding to me and my staff, is that clear?

I said nothing, did nothing.

What we have to do is administer a full physical examination to you in order to make sure you are in a suitable condition for us to have a look at your brain. That may sound a little frightening, but it's completely painless.

What's going to happen is you're going to be taken to an examination room down the hall. In that room there will be a paper gown. We are going to need you to take off all your clothing and put the paper gown on. Then Nancy will come back and do the assessment. We need to be sure that you are healthy, and if you're not healthy, we can find a way to get you to be healthy. And we need to understand what sort of person you are—do you understand? Do you understand what I mean by that?

I looked instinctively toward the wall as if I might find a window there, but the room, I had forgotten, was windowless. I suddenly felt heavy, that I could not move even if I tried, that there was no way for me to lift myself from this chair.

For instance, I can do the assessment myself if you're more comfortable with a man than a woman doing the physical. It's your choice, and remember—this is the part without your clothing, so which will it be? A man or woman?

I had not thought so much about the clothing on my body,

had not questioned where it had come from or what it was. The shirt and pants were made from the same thick material, something almost like canvas, a gray-black-brown—it depended on the light. There was one square pocket on the shirt, several pockets on the pants, and a loop for holding some sort of tool I'd never had.

So I assume you're all right with a woman doing the assessment then? Unless you speak up now, I can only make assumptions about what you might be thinking . . .

Dr. Winslow was silent for some time, then there was a knock and Nancy was there and we were all walking down a hallway and at the end of the hallway was a door with a little window in it and beyond the window I could see a bit of lawn before a thicket of trees. There was a large red bar across this door and a sign: EMERGENCY EXIT ONLY.

Nancy opened a door on the left side of the hall and let me into a small room with nothing in it but a padded examination table. At the edge of the table was a paper gown folded in a square. I stood still in the room but I was not in the room. I looked at the paper gown but I could not see it. I thought of the emergency exit.

Nancy told me to remove all my clothing—*socks, underwear, all of it*—and put on the paper gown and she'd be back in just a moment to do the examination. My face must have said something I couldn't hide; she told me there was no reason to be afraid, that it wouldn't hurt, that it would only take a few minutes. *I'll be back when you're ready*, she said, and shut the door.

I looked at the gown, looked down at my shoes, plain black

ones with thick soles and no laces. I listened at the door, heard her footsteps disappearing, then nothing, then nothing, then nothing. I held my ear to the door—still, nothing. I put my hand on the knob, tried to turn it, but it would not turn. I thought of the hallway, thought of the emergency exit at the hallway's end, the trees beyond the emergency exit, and wondered what sort of trees they were and how much shade they might offer. I knew about trees, but I didn't know anything about this.

I sat on the cushioned examination table beside the folded gown. My shoes were still on my feet, clothes still on this body. I leaned back across the table and shut my eyes and thought that at some point in the future, long after humanity had run its course, after some other creature had replaced us, maybe, or maybe even after the next creatures had been replaced by whatever came after them, at some point in a future I could not fully imagine, a question might occur in some mind, and that question might be *What was the human? What was the world of the human?*—though it would be in some unforeseen language, perhaps a language that was without sound, perhaps a language that did not have to grow from a damp, contaminated mouth— and if this question ever did arise in that future being's mind, would it even be possible to catalog and make sense of all our griefs, our pains and wars? Our delineations? Our need for order? The question arose then—did all this human trouble begin in our bodies, these failing things, weaker or stronger, lighter or darker, taller or shorter? Why did they cause so much trouble for us? Why did we use them against one another? Why did we think the content of a body meant anything? Why did we draw our conclusions with our bodies when the body is so inconclusive, so mercurial?

Resting on that table, not getting undressed, not putting on the paper gown, I feared I'd become something sacrificial, but I would not lay myself out on this altar. Whatever else I may have been, I was, I knew, not theirs.

The door opened and Nancy was there, somehow leaning toward and away from me at once—

Well, I guess I nearly forgot about you down here—or not exactly forgot, but we just had a few people show up and . . . well, everything is sort of confusing here the past few days.

She stood shaking her head, frowning at the clipboard in her hands.

Well, where were we?

She flipped through the papers on the clipboard, then looked up.

Goodness me—you haven't even gotten undressed! Now, how am I supposed to do the examination if you're still in all your clothes and all? I'll just give you another minute, then, OK? We haven't got all day you know—

She shut the door and I heard her footsteps going rapidly back down the hall. I sat up, tested the door again—still locked. A tiny noise—something like the sound of a leaking ceiling, a drop of water clicking against tile, then silence, another sound, silence, another. I ran my hands across the ground, looking for water, but found, between a chair's leg and the wall—an insect the size of my smallest fingernail. It was something like a grasshopper but smaller and brown. It jumped every few seconds, but landed on its back, the hard shell ticking against the floor.

I caught it softly in my hands—one of its hind legs was bent the wrong way. It kept my attention. I could not think in any other direction.

Nancy and Dr. Winslow must have come in at some point, but I did not notice until they were standing close, standing over me and asking question after question.

When I looked up at them, they stopped speaking and the silence around all of us was the sort that comes after something has shattered—a clear, high silence.

See? Nancy said to Dr. Winslow. *And we don't have enough staff to deal with an uncooperative patient.* Dr. Winslow nodded, turned, and was gone.

OUTSIDE THE HOSPITAL I crouched beside a bush, opened my cupped hands, and waited for the insect to jump out. I felt Hilda's shadow cast across my back. The insect did not move. I looked for its eye or antennae to flicker, but they did not. Its legs were bent up into its body. I set it down in some mulch beneath the bush and stood, uncertain.

Hilda did not speak as we got into the car or as the car left the parking lot or as the car sped up the ramp to the highway, down the highway, miles down the highway, taking us with it. She did not speak and she did not turn on the radio. She did not look at me and I did not look at her. We both looked forward and wet, cold gusts of air came through the vents toward us. I wondered about the insect, about whether it was dead, whether I might have suffocated it, whether I had crushed it somehow without realizing.

I'm a patient woman, Hilda said eventually. *I was taught to be patient, and I am patient, and I believe Jesus would be patient, so it's what I should do and I really do try, but I am just about running out of patience.*

She opened her palms on the steering wheel then regripped it, finger by finger, faint veins visible along her forearms.

I'm sorry, but . . . the examination—maybe we didn't make it clear or maybe I didn't make it clear—this was important to us.

Steven and I decided that we really needed some clarity on you in order to keep you in our house. We have concerns, you know, legitimate concerns. And this lack of cooperation, well, it is really trying my patience. We can't help you if you won't tell us anything and won't even let a doctor make sure you're physically . . . all right. You must understand that we're not obligated to help you—that we're doing this out of our own kindness. And who do you think paid for that? I paid for that. It's not free. They're not just giving out free doctors' appointments to anyone who needs them, you know. We had to pay for it, and it wasn't cheap.

Some distance up the highway a small car appeared to have driven off into a ditch. A tow truck was there. A few people stood at the edge of the road, still and close together while someone attached a chain to the back of the car.

You must think I've never known anything hard, that none of us do, that we could never understand. But isn't that just the problem? We don't know anything about you because you won't tell us, but we're only asking so we can help you.

Hilda slowed down as we approached the car and truck. A woman was sitting on the side of the road, at the feet of two men. Her hair was matted on one side with what looked like blood. The men stood with their arms folded, watching as the chain went taut and slowly pulled the car from the ditch. As we passed them, Hilda rolled down her window and stuck an arm out, waving. All three of them waved back, waved and smiled, even the one with the bloody head. Hilda rolled her window up and sped away.

Maybe you think we won't understand, but we really would understand. I know difficulty. I know real pain. She swallowed.

I'll even tell you. Then she didn't say anything. We drove a half mile in silence before she began.

My father, the man you met in the waiting room, a few years ago he was real sick, nearly died, and after that he just wasn't the same anymore. Then one afternoon, he got a kitchen knife and stabbed my stepmother in the eye. Just stabbed her in the eye, just like that out of nowhere. So we had to put him out there at Monroe because the nursing home wouldn't take him and thank God he didn't manage to kill Paulina because our family—our reputation—well, I don't think we would have recovered from something like that. It would have affected me, the boys, my husband. We would have all been tainted, maybe would've been forced to move away . . .

When my father married Paulina, well, she was so much younger than him and she didn't—she just didn't match *the rest of us. She was nervous and she looked different, you know, dark haired, sort of tan—well . . . She never knew her father and I think there was a reason her mother kept him hidden. She didn't even wear white at the wedding—and it wasn't her second wedding or anything. You can't even imagine how difficult it was growing up. Even at church the children picked on me about it. Seems like children are often the first to just come out and say what's wrong with something. And to have to call someone Mother who behaves like she did . . . Well, it just wasn't right. We were the only family like that in town, so we had to work twice as hard to be . . . right. To sit right with the community. It's all we have here—sitting right with the community. It's all anyone wants.*

Of course—Mrs. Gladstone, Paulina—she's clearly never been the same and bless her heart she's all self-conscious about that glass eye. Won't hardly ever go out. I try to include her, you know, in my life. I don't want her to be so abandoned but she won't even leave her house, ever—just won't leave, and I can hardly set a foot in there.

And when she woke up in the hospital she thought her husband— my father—she was so sure that he *was the one who was dead, and no matter what we told her, no matter how many times we explained that he was alive, that he had attacked her, she just didn't believe it. She thinks it was her fault she lost that eye, and she kept saying,* No, my Charles wouldn't do something like that. It must have been some strange man, some strange man that came in, then blamed it on Charlie. *I told her, no, it wasn't some strange man, that Charles had even admitted himself that he'd done it. And she just kept saying that if it was really him, then she must have done something to* deserve *it. Can you imagine?*

I remembered Paulina, Mrs. Gladstone, sitting quietly in her house, still and alone. The human mind is so easily bent, and so uneasily smoothed.

I was the one who found her, Hilda said. *She'd staggered out onto her front porch, gushing blood, and thank God I drove by when I did or she would have died right there on her lawn, and then what would we have done? Wouldn't have been anything to do then but move away or something . . .*

On the highway ahead of us you could see the heat rising, warping the air. Hilda unwrapped two sticks of chewing gum, put them in her mouth, and chewed as she spoke.

All I am saying is that I know a thing or two about going through something difficult. That's all I'm saying. So maybe there's something you don't want to talk about, but you've got to talk about it. That's the only way things get better. It's the only way. You could at least think about what it might be like for us, for our community.

We don't know what to do, and there you are showing up in the middle of the festival week plus all this confusion going on over in Almose County. It's an especially difficult moment and we need you to cooperate. Do you understand?

Hilda stopped and turned off the car in the driveway beside Roger's house, but she didn't open her door so I didn't open mine and we sat there for awhile. A few times Hilda began to speak, got two or three words out before stopping, then starting again. She kept looking straight ahead out the windshield, so I did, too.

Roger is going to take you over to visit a friend of his for the day, and I need to talk to Steven about whether you can keep staying with us. He may think and I might think that it's just too much for us, for the family, the boys. And it is—well . . .

She started to open her door but stopped and shut it again, turning to me, her face softer and voice brightened and high.

But I just want you to know that you really are welcome in our house—you're welcome there and I really do mean that. I don't have any problem with you, *exactly, and I really do want the best for you and you must know that if we can't have you stay with us anymore that it isn't a personal decision—it's a practical one. And I mean it, you really are welcome in my home at any time in the future, and you have been welcome all this time and I want you to know that. It's just I'll have to see what Steven says is the most practical. After today and everything. I just have to see what he thinks.*

She nodded to her own faint reflection in the windshield.

MOST PEOPLE AROUND HERE are not fond of strangers, you know. I probably don't need to tell you.

Tammy was smoking a thin cigarette, ashing into an empty soda can. The house was wooden and old, all its planks buckling and splintered, pale blue paint chipping. Through the neglect, it was clear this place had been cared for in other ways. Roger had left me there an hour before, saying only that he would be back later.

No, she said, taking a long drag on the thin cigarette, *I probably don't need to tell you that at all.*

She and I sat together on the porch, listening. Every half hour or so a train roared down the train tracks behind the house, a wall of metal noise, suddenly there and large, then fading, then gone. Sometimes I watched her cigarettes disappear into breath, but most of the time I just stared at the yard overtaken by tangled vines and dead leaves. Some cats were in there, rustling round, trying to kill anything they could.

You know—I would have never thought I'd be one of those wives who waited all afternoon for her husband to get back from work, but maybe it's true that you just turn into your mother— whether you notice or not, you ain't got a choice.

She smiled at this, shook her head, then dropped her cigarette into the soda can. It hissed in the can's wet.

Bless her. The bitch. I shouldn't speak ill of the dead, I know, but . . . well, people shouldn't speak ill of their own children either. I suppose I—well, I guess I disappointed her too much and she didn't live long enough to burn off all that disappointment.

A tabby came up the porch steps with a corpse swaying from his mouth, but Tammy laid a firm look on him; he paused midstep, retreated slowly, then bolted back into the yard's overgrowth.

Did you have parents or just some people who thought they should own somebody?

Neither, I said. The word took me by surprise, came out abrupt and soft.

Huh. Orphan?

I didn't say anything for a while, looked at the wooden floor, felt a memory lingering in me somewhere, like someone uncertain at a front door, hesitating at the bell. *I don't remember.*

Well. It's overrated, family. You're lucky if you get born into one where you belong. It's really a lot more rare than people want to say. You know, I ran off to the city when I was—Jesus . . . was I seventeen? Well, we know how that story ends, don't we?

She swallowed hard and lit another cigarette.

But the thing is—I found a place to sleep for a few weeks, way out in some neighborhood, I couldn't even tell you where it was now—I was in way over my dumb head. But it was a Latvian neighborhood and I got a little job sweeping up hair at this beauty parlor owned by this old Latvian lady—I can't even remember her name now, that's how stupid I am. I mean, I don't even think I'd even heard of Latvia—I was just real dumb. Still am. But she was so nice to me, and so funny, and I was just this ugly little girl with no money, no friends, and I hadn't done anything or seen anything. She'd had such a different life—leaving her country, leaving everyone she ever knew, really starting over—but I felt I had more in common with her than anyone I'd grown up with, more than anyone I'd known down here, more than my own family. Immediately, I felt it. I can't explain why. I don't know why it is a person can feel so misplaced, even from the beginning, you know—even as a little child I felt there had been some kind of accident that got me born here. I guess my mother, the whole family, really, felt the same way, that there had been some sort of mistake. And now where am I? Ten miles from where I was born, puttering around all day, napping and smoking too much and trying not to eat the whole kitchen.

She stubbed out her cigarette and sat still and quietly for a while.

I don't mean to be so negative. I know that's not what people like. Sometimes it's just hard to really think about your life, all the years of it you can't take back, to think about what it is.

For a long time we waited for that last sentence to vanish, and when it seemed it had gotten far enough away from us, she stood up and began pacing the porch.

I'm not going to tell, she said over her shoulder. *That you said something. You know that's what everyone wants, don't you? That's what they're waiting on? Some of them think you're a mute, of course, that it's medical, nothing to be done anything about, and you may as well let them keep thinking that. Me and Hal won't rat you out to nobody. Maybe nobody'd believe us anyway.* She leaned over the porch railing, maybe looking for the cat, then she turned around—*This place, you know, it's not so terrible, but it's not so nice either.*

She crouched to turn on a small radio on the floor. Someone was singing with a piano and Tammy sang along in a small, half-embarrassed way. A red car drove up and parked in the one part of the yard where the vines and roots had been cut back. A slight man emerged from the car and climbed the porch steps, smiling at Tammy all the while. He wore a green shirt with the name HAL on a patch sewn over his heart. When she embraced Hal, Tammy seemed almost twice his height—she had to hunch to kiss the top of his bald head. They touched each other so naturally, so easily, it was as if each of them had a kind of wind vane tuned for the other.

Name's Hal. He smiled and waved one hand sharply at me. He sat on the old sofa where Tammy had been. She'd gone inside the house but soon came back out with a bowl of potato chips and a dark red drink for him, ice singing in the glass. I was staring at a few large and brightly colored feathers that hung above us, spinning in the ceiling-fan draft.

You ever seen a peacock? Hal asked.

Oh, here we go. Tammy lit a cigarette and paced at the edge of the porch.

Vaguely, I sensed a memory of waking up on a lawn somewhere and seeing two large birds—peacocks—staring at me from across the grass. One of them spread out a great tail of feathers, and the other did the same. They swayed there, necks long and twitching. Each feather seemed to be watching me for a moment, watching me through the silence and heat, then they'd closed up those fans and darted away, dragging all that finery across the grass, running for their lives.

Pretty things, Hal said. *Tammy always liked them so I saved up to have some out here. They came mail order, came in a crate shipped overnight. They were just so beautiful. I couldn't hardly believe it—bright blue, sort of purple at some angles. Real pretty like that. But, anyway—what we did was put them in the old chicken coop, which had just been sitting empty since we built the new one, but by the next morning something had gotten in there and ate up two of 'em, blood and all those blue feathers all over the lawn, and Tammy—sweet one that she is—she went around collecting the feathers, just crying and picking up feathers.*

I'm using some of them to make something, Tammy said. *In their memory. I don't know what yet, but they were just too beautiful to go to waste, rotting into the ground like that.*

Anyway we moved what was left of the peacocks to the new chicken coop while we tried to fix up the old one, Hal said. *I guessed maybe a wild dog or something had ripped into it. I figured that the peacocks would be just fine in the coop with the hens for a while.*

I hate this part, Tammy said to herself, pacing the longest edge of the porch. *We should have known better.*

They're all birds, Hal said, *so I didn't think there'd be a problem. And it did seem all right at first because all the hens piled up to one side of the coop, piled on each other like a bunch of dogs or something, afraid of them peacocks, really, but before I knew it, the biggest hen in there found the littlest peacock and pecked the damn thing near to death. I don't know what came over that bird—I still don't know—though it just about made me believe in some kind of evil spirit or something—I mean, I'd just never seen a hen so riled up, making these weird gurgling noises, running real fast—so fast that I couldn't even catch the damn thing to slit its throat—had to use the rifle. Imagine that—shooting a hen. Bullet tore that little thing right up. Pretty much ruined it.*

Well, I wasn't going to cook it anyway, Tammy said, *even if you'd slit its throat like regular—I wasn't going to eat that bird.*

It sure did seem to be some kind of evil—that's all I was saying. It wasn't—well, I don't know . . . I don't know what it was or wasn't. Not really. Not for certain.

I made him bury it over on the other side of the tracks, Tammy said. *I didn't want that thing near me.* She smoked and stared out at the yard. Where do people go when that kind of look comes over them?

So after I buried the hen, I put the last three peacocks in a cage in a fenced-off part of the garden so that nothing else *could get to it—none of our animals, nobody's dog, no wild animals, nothing. And wouldn't you just know? Out of nowhere this storm swept in, lightning and everything, some hail even, and two of them got drowned and the last one was left shaking under the other two dead ones, and that last one, well, he held on for a week or so till someone stole him or he just up and left.*

I bet he ran off. It was just nothing but hell here for those birds, Tammy said. *I feel bad about it all the time, every day.*

You didn't mean no harm.

I wanted peacocks all my life, ever since I was little. Her eyes were glassing over. She lit another cigarette as she spoke. *Then as soon as I finally get them, I go and mess it all up.*

It just wasn't meant to be. You didn't do no harm, Tams.

But I did!

You didn't.

Indirectly, I did.

Well, I don't know about—

It's just as bad—indirectly. Just as bad. Maybe even worse. I should have known more about how you keep them. I didn't—I just didn't—

She raised a limp hand to her face and shook beneath it.

Oh, Tammy. You couldn't have known. I didn't bring it up to make you upset, Tams. It's been years now and I was just thinking of them. There's all sorts of things a person can't know till it's too late.

A train passed us, seeming louder and longer than the others. When it was gone, I noticed a little cricket at the edge of the porch, chirping, and I wanted to say something to Tammy and Hal, wanted to tell them what I was thinking, what I felt, but the words were all out of reach. The words were not mine to use. I wished I knew how to make a sound the way an insect does. I wish everyone knew how to speak that way, just that one word, no language at all.

After a while, Hal said, *it starts to seem like that train is always there, don't it? That it's always there only there are just times you can hear it. Don't it seem that way to you? Like the whole house is always rattling, all the time?*

Tammy smiled at him and sat on the porch steps, facing the weedy yard full of cats. None of us spoke for some time. Sunlight began to leave. Another train went by.

WOULDN'T YOU LIKE TO COME ON IN? Tammy asked from the door.

Moths were clustered around the porch light. A television was speaking somewhere in the house.

It's nice and cool in here now and you can have a Coke. She was still standing in the mouth between house and porch, nowhere. Only then did I realize that I was alone in the dark out there, though I couldn't account for the minutes that had just passed, couldn't remember Hal and Tammy leaving. As I looked at Tammy, a train went by, its noise massive, and I felt sure, at once, that Tammy had the ability to tolerate an enormous amount of pain before she let anyone know.

All right, well, I can't make you do nothing, she said then, quietly—*nobody can make you do nothing.*

The window behind me sent down a square of yellow light at my feet. Shadows flicked through it sometimes, or it sat still and flat. The voice of a television; infinite purring insects; a light bulb hissed. A car drove up and parked some distance from the house. Headlights on then off. Two doors opened, shut. The sound of feet carrying themselves through loose stones. Roger and Nelson emerged from the darkness and up the stairs.

Nice night, Roger said, as Nelson walked straight into the house without a word left behind him. *Well, I guess someone's in a hurry.*

A rocking chair creaked as Roger lowered himself into it.

Did you have a nice day with Tammy?

I nodded. Roger rocked in his chair, half-lit, half in darkness, tapping his foot in an unsteady rhythm for a while.

Well. I heard how it went with Dr. Winslow, so I guess I'm probably not your favorite person right now for setting that up . . .

His fingers were tangled together, prone on his lap. Inside the house I could hear Tammy asking questions that Nelson blunted with one-word replies.

I usually don't like to be too personal, Roger said, *not to project too much onto someone, but it's difficult for me not to—see something of myself in . . . your being here. You know, it's probably no surprise, but I'm sort of a little bit different from most people here. I'm not like Steven, for instance, not like Hal. It's not a secret really. I don't know what people might say about me when I'm not around. Maybe it's nice, maybe it's not so nice. But no one acts ugly to me. Not to my face. They let me alone. I do my work and it all suits me fine. Of course people do talk a lot—they probably gossip, I don't know—but if they do, it's just behind closed doors. Only then. They're polite like that.*

Moths fluttered toward and away from the light and we watched them. A few times Roger turned his shoulders somewhat toward me, but his eyes were fixed upward, on the light, away.

I'm not saying that you're like me, but if you're being so quiet because you're afraid that you're too different from other people, then I don't think you have anything to be worried about. It's probably not as bad here as you might expect.

He laughed lightly, but only for a moment, and when I looked at him, I could see the part of Roger that never moved. Too much light will blind you and too much water will drown you. It is a danger to accept anything real from another person, to know something of them. A person has to be careful about the voices they listen to, the faces they let themselves see.

Roger stood quickly, began pacing as his tone became lifting and light; the pressure of the moment fell away like a shrugged-off coat.

Tammy and Hal, they're very progressive, you know. That's why I thought you might like to visit with them. People thought maybe you'd relate to Tammy, since she's . . . well, since she's Tammy. Long time ago they had a child, adopted of course because—well—anyway, it's a sad story and since then they keep dogs and chickens and I think they used to keep peacocks over here, too, or I thought they did. And everyone thought it would be good for you and Nelson to visit again. Then after dinner I'll take you back to Hilda and Steven's place—so, that's the plan. You'll stay with them again . . . everyone decided that was the best. Consistency. That sort of thing.

Tammy came out onto the porch and lit a cigarette. She was wearing an apron and her hair was tied up in a blue bandanna. *Roger, is there anything*—but she stopped herself, looked toward the window, came closer to Roger, and lowered her voice—*is there anything Nelson won't eat? I tried asking him but he wasn't saying much but I just thought there are rules about*

*what they can eat—aren't there? Like kosher but something else—
what's the word for it?*

*Oh, I think he just eats whatever at this point. He's been here for
a while and they didn't tell me anything when I called about him.*

Tammy nodded, stood up straight, and took a long vanish-
ing drag from her cigarette. *Huh*, she said. *Well, I guess that's
good because we're having chicken-fried pork chops and I just didn't
even think about it until he got here and I saw him and thought,
Oh, no—I forgot to ask about that . . . boy.*

When we went inside, Hal and Nelson were watching the
television, Nelson gripping the soft limbs of his armchair and
Hal smoking a pipe. On the television a teenage girl was being
interviewed, her face collapsing into tears, reopening to speak,
collapsing again. On the screen below—ALMOSE COUNTY IN
CRISIS.

We should probably turn that off about now, Tammy shouted as
she passed through the room toward the kitchen, *don't you think?*

Reckon so. Hal hesitated for a moment, then stood and
aimed the remote at the screen. A heavy quiet fell on the room.

Put on a record—don't you think we should put on a record?
Tammy asked from the kitchen. Hal didn't answer, just moved
through the room, then put his pipe between his teeth, freeing
both hands to slide a record from its sleeve.

I know I shouldn't—he said through a clenched jaw—*and
before dinner and all, but, man alive*—he took the pipe from
his mouth, set the needle on the record—*everything is just so
strange lately*—a woman began to sing—*I can't help but smoke
like a goddamn barbecue.*

109

Roger started to say something, then stopped, started, then stopped again. *I don't know, but I just—no . . . no . . . Never mind.*

Times like these—well, I keep thinking about evilness—

Yes, exactly, Roger said.

Anyway, we were both just about to quit with the smoking, you know, and had even planned last week that this was the week we'd cut down, but now—well, I just can't. Or I haven't. Or I don't want to. Can't seem to do anything right these days.

Roger nodded, looked at his hands in his lap. Nelson was looking around the room, looking into one corner, then another.

And this time of year, what with Saturday coming up and all . . . I mean, I keep having this feeling that I'm glad it's happening in Almose and not here—ain't that a mean thought? Hal looked up at the ceiling fan, held his pipe in one hand, and squinted. *Glad about someone's suffering because at least it ain't your own.*

Softly I gripped the back of my other hand, that forgotten place where the knuckles grow. Tammy called us into the dining room and directed us each to a seat at the table. Hal said a blessing and the table went quiet with eating until Tammy said, *Oh, isn't this nice? The two of you, new friends. It's just so nice to see. I think it's great.*

Great, Nelson said, *uh-huh.* As a train roared by, Tammy caught a spider with a glass and newspaper, then went outside to release it.

She's always doing that sort of thing, Hal said to us, the train howling farther from us now. *Letting bugs out of the house like that.* He shook his head. *They're just going to come back in, I tell her, but she ain't having it.*

After dinner Nelson and I were given two bowls of ice cream, a deck of cards, and told to go out back and entertain ourselves. As soon as the back door shut, Nelson pulled a metal flask from his pocket, took a swig, poured some over his ice cream, and passed it to me.

The metal was skin warmed—I could have cried—but I just repeated the long sip and pour, just as he'd done it. The last drops, pale brown, fell over the ice cream like rusted water into a basin.

You know where I get it? The whiskey?

I shook my head.

Butch gives it to me. He keeps me stocked. I keep thinking it's because he feels sorry that we both have to put up with Kitty. She wants me to call her Mom but I won't. My mom's dead, *I told her one time, and she started crying, and Butch told her to stop and I said something about how she didn't even know my mom, and why would she cry about someone she doesn't know, but she just cried more, then she got mad and got up in my face, so Butch made her go upstairs and started giving me this, whatever it is, bourbon. Anyway this afternoon Kitty tells me I'm going to see my new friend. And I say,* Who? *And she says,* Pew, your friend. *And, I mean—no offense—but we are not friends. Not to me. I mean, I don't know you. You don't know me. So I tell her,* How can Pew be my friend? *We don't even know each other. And she says something about how we all need to be welcoming to you, and anyway that you and me must have a lot in common. And I say,* Because we're both brown? *Must seem all the same to her. And you know what? She fucking laughs. She didn't even answer me at all. Just laughed. But now that I see you again—I don't know—you seemed darker the other day. It's weird . . . Never mind. I mean, I don't care. I don't give a shit.*

He started dealing the cards into stacks. One for me. One for him. One in the center. *I mean, it's fine. We're cool. But it doesn't matter to me if we hang out or not—and I don't think we have anything in common really. Not really. Other than not being from here.*

Nelson set a king down between us. Two heads. Four hands. A king. *I'm not even doing anything here—I don't know any card games. Guess you don't either?*

I shook my head.

Figures. We continued setting cards atop other cards, cards in pairs and alone. Taking cards and discarding cards, making order, making chaos, shuffling. An hour passed like this. Nelson produced a second flask from the ankle of his boot. We drank it, finished it. I softened into the night.

It became clear we had invented a game by accident, all the rules unspoken. We each won and lost. We spanned some time together. When a train passed, we pressed our hands over the table to protect it from the gust. Somehow we both knew what it all meant, what the game meant, what it was for.

I had this dream the other night, Nelson said, *do you want to hear about it?*

He swept all the cards together, then shuffled and redealt them, not looking at me, then stopping to look at me.

I only ask because people think other people's dreams are boring. Do you? Do you think other people's dreams are boring?

No.

Me either—not if it's a good one anyway. Anyway—it was one of those dreams that you're not in, it's just something you're watching happen to other people. And it was this meeting or something, all these scientists and philosophers are there, giving speeches—I guess it's sort of what I imagine college could be like. All these experts and stuff. And there's this one person there who decided to change her body into a horse's body. Like—she decided that she would only be happy if she could change herself into a horse. And she's spent her whole life inventing these drugs and surgeries to turn herself into an animal, and little by little she's changed herself into a horse and this conference is . . . maybe it's like the first time she's publicly being a horse. But something about the surgery meant that she had to become a baby horse first, and her skin is almost translucent—have you ever seen a newborn horse?

I shook my head.

Well, she really looks like one, maybe even a premature one, and she can't even walk yet, so someone is pushing her around in a wheelbarrow and also she can't talk but she's invented this device that turns her thoughts into words for her, so that's how she's giving a lecture about this thing she's done to herself. And she's saying that she might later change into a different animal, then a different one, and that it's a way to keep living a longer and longer life—because this woman, for some reason I know that she's maybe sixty or seventy or something. Like, super old. And also, in the dream, I sort of knew that it was a controversy, that some people thought it was not right of her to do this, but everyone that was there was just listening to her talk through this speaker thing . . . out of the wheelbarrow.

Nelson put down a ten of clubs onto the stack and for some

reason he stopped talking and we resumed putting our cards out on top of one another, taking and giving.

I mean, I can't stop thinking about it, but it's not that big of a deal. It's just a weird dream. I keep thinking about that lady and I keep thinking—you know, she's right and everyone else is wrong. I don't even know why I bring it up—probably just playing cards reminded me for some reason. Roger told me when you have a dream it's just about you and you—that all the characters in the dream are just parts of you, talking to each other. But—I don't know. It don't matter or anything.

We were quiet for a minute, then Nelson won a round of our invented game.

I just thought it was funny, he said. *Or stupid or something. I had the dream like a month ago, way before you even showed up, just so you know. So it's not about you. I don't care what you are. It doesn't make any difference to me.*

As Roger drove us away from Tammy and Hal's place, down curving dark roads and empty fields, the moon was there, same moon as ever, hiding behind thin clouds. Nelson got out of the car without saying goodbye, taking slow, short steps toward the monstrous house that kept him. I watched him, not knowing when I'd see him again. Roger shouted something after him, some kind of thanks or concern, and Nelson threw his arm up—a dismissal, a goodbye.

When we got to Hilda and Steven's house, Roger turned to me, his mouth hesitating at a word. He started to reach out to touch my shoulder but put his hand on the edge of the passenger seat and said, *It's . . . um, I really think it's all going to work out just fine.*

Steven was on the porch, drinking from a silver can. As I came up the stairs, he stood, opened the front door, and shouted inside—

Hilda!

I stood still on the porch stairs. Nothing for a moment. Then footsteps coming from somewhere in the house.

Go on inside for a minute, Steven said to me. *Hilda and I just have to talk for a minute, then we'd like to speak to you before bed. There's cold drinks in the kitchen.*

I drank lukewarm water from the kitchen faucet, then went to the room where the parrot lived. It was hunched on one side of the cage, its feathers flared the same way hair rises from a cold body. I sat in the armchair beside the cage and looked out the window for a while, looked at all the plants in the dark.

The kingdom of God is within you—the parrot said. *The kingdom of God is within you. Within you. Within you. Fuck you. Fuck you. The kingdom of God.*

A little laughter came from across the room.

What'd you do to piss him off like that, huh? Jack asked. I could see a smile of white teeth faintly through the unlit room.

Fuck you, the bird said. *Fuck you. Fuck you. The kingdom of God. The kingdom of God.*

Jack kept laughing, stood and came over to the cage, opened it and took the parrot out, put it on his shoulder and stared down at me. Just as he began to say something, the front door opened and Steven shouted in—

Jack, go back to bed. How many times do I have to—

You forgot to feed Little Chuck, so I was just feeding him. Dad, he's hungry—

Steven stomped down the hall toward us, grabbed the parrot from Jack's shoulder and threw it back into the cage. The parrot flapped around the cage saying, *Fine, how are you? Fine, how are you?*

If you are not asleep in five minutes, Steven said, *you are in huge trouble.*

Jack retreated, no longer laughing, disappeared down a hall, and slammed a door.

Hilda and I would like to talk to you on the porch for a minute. Steven threw a handful of birdseed into the cage.

From the porch I watched moths hover around a tall lamp across the street. Others flew helplessly against the screens that kept Steven and Hilda and me away from them.

When we said you could stay with us as long as you needed, we really did mean that and we still mean it, Steven began. Hilda nodded.

We do.

And we're still not sure about how to include you in the festival. Do you remember us telling you about it?

I nodded, but I was still thinking about Nelson's dream, and wondering why it was that anyone believed the human body needed to be any particular way, or what was so important about a human body. Was it possible for a human's mind and history and memory and ideas to live inside the body of a horse, and if it was, did that make that being a human or a horse? What difference did it make, one life or another?

Well, Steven and I consulted quite a few people about whether or not we should have you attend . . . or even participate in the festival. You know—it's really something we do only for ourselves, and we're concerned it wouldn't make sense or would even be . . . well—

It's just that we introduce the festival to children over the course of a few years, Steven said, *we ease them into it.*

Yes, Hilda said faintly, almost to herself. *And we're just not sure what could happen if you . . . well, if you don't get eased into it.*

I believe it will make sense once you're there, Steven said, *or at least once it's all over. It hasn't really been decided how much we need to explain beforehand. It may sound . . . well . . . it may sound stranger than it actually is.*

It's really very normal, Hilda said. *And useful.*

Yes.

But that's not until Saturday and there is, like we said, no need to worry about it right now.

We just wanted to prepare you, Steven said.

Tomorrow there's going to be a reception at Kitty and Butch's house—you know, Nelson's family—it's during the school day, so the kids won't be there, but many people are very much looking forward to meeting you . . .

Yes. Our community is very eager to find every possible way we can to help you move forward in your life, whether that means you'll be integrated here or whether there might be some other place that might be more appropriate and comfortable for you.

And we're just going to have a little reception, some of us from the church, to discuss our ideas, Hilda said. *Really, the whole thing will be so casual, it's not really a big deal at all. We just thought it was the right thing to do, get everyone on the same page, put our heads together, that sort of thing.*

And we do remember how we promised you could stay with us as long as you need, and of course we are serious about that promise, however, it's possible you might not need *to stay with us anymore, and should that be the case, we will wish you well, wherever you go.*

Yes . . . Yes. Hilda nodded in a tiny, silent agreement with Steven.

And if you do move on to live elsewhere, we want you to understand it's not because we don't want you to live here. It would simply be a matter of what is best for you. What is decided to be best for you.

Hilda was looking at the floor with a strange trouble on her face.

Well, Steven said. *Time for everyone to get some rest.*

We all went inside, and as I reached the top of the attic stairs, I heard Steven begin to speak so I turned to him. *We just wish you would say something, that's all. We really do wish that. We really do.*

I heard the door lock low behind me.

THURSDAY

I WAS SITTING by the little round window watching the tree branches when I heard the attic door unlock and footsteps on the stairs. Hilda appeared, eased into the room.

Now, I'm not sure that, uh—well . . . there's this neighbor of ours who has been asking to see you ever since Sunday and I just thought you might have had enough visiting with people, so I told him I just didn't think there was time but . . . well, he just insists. Normally I would put my foot down, but Mr. Kercher is a very quiet man and he usually doesn't take to insisting on anything. His daughter married the Hindmans' boy, so he retired here—can't remember where from—and he's a real nice neighbor—set up this nature trail over there in the woods last year and he wants to take you on a walk through it? You don't have to go, but if you'd like, he's here and we don't have to be anywhere until after lunch.

Mr. Kercher stood on the front porch holding his hat.

The morning is cool, he said. *Unusually cool, but not for long. Therefore, I will go for a walk in the little woods we have here. Would you join me?*

I nodded and followed him away from the house, down the sidewalk, toward a shadowy cluster of pines at the end of the block. We were silent as we went. Several times I thought Mr. Kercher was about to say something, but he gave up before a word came.

The pines were narrow and sparse. A path had been patted down between them. Every few paces, there was a stone on which someone had painted little white arrows to guide the way.

Hello, Mr. Kercher said, stooping to pet a pile of green moss. He looked at the moss the way I'd seen people look at children or babies sleeping in strollers, soft bodies someone larger had to protect. *Goodbye*, he said just as quietly and seriously as before. He stood again and we kept walking.

Where I am from, we have many woods, many hikers. Here, not so many—people go to church instead. So we must let the forest know we appreciate it.

We kept walking, slowly, each step soft. A few feet off the path a dark bird was bathing in a puddle. She turned her beak toward Mr. Kercher as we passed, chirped, then flew deeper into the woods. We climbed a slight hill, and when we reached the top, the light shifted, made the world more stark and clear. There was a log on its side and Mr. Kercher sat, so I sat next to him and we listened to a creek below us, listened to the water pass over the stones and the stones be washed with water. A wind came and went.

In our silence I felt as if something had been given back to me that I'd lost a long time ago. Mr. Kercher did not look at me and I did not look at him. There was no need.

I feel . . . confused all the time, Mr. Kercher said eventually. *My daughter, Ava, says it is because I am getting old. I know I am getting old. It may be the only natural form of justice. Maybe. But I do not think my confusion has to do with aging.*

I moved here because I love my daughter and she is all I have left. She got married. They have three children. He is—his whole family is from here. It seems his family, the Hindmans, has some special . . . distinction in the town. They are—they have been kind to me, but I do not understand this reverence. I fear it is only because they are wealthy. I've seen people line up to talk to one of them, and there are special tables at restaurants, lots of invitations to things. The Hindmans are on all these boards, these groups of people who make decisions about other people. Perhaps there is something I do not know about them, but I have been here for many years and . . . well . . . I don't want to speak ill of them. The Hindmans have been perfectly nice to me. Or at least they have not been rude. And Ava chose to join this family, to become a Hindman, so I must respect her choice. Everyone has their own life, their own decisions, and anyway, so much is outside our control—the circumstances of our deaths and births, that is, and the various circumstances that pass between those times—

As I listened to Mr. Kercher, I was visited by a memory or the memory of an old dream—of an autumn afternoon when I was sitting on a bench in a town square somewhere. One of the storefronts nearby had several white gowns in the window, sequined and lacy and draped on headless mannequins, and the square was quiet, no sounds but a far-off church bell or a clock chime, until a young woman ran out of that store, the door bursting open and several other women pursuing her. The young woman was wearing a loose pale blue slip and screaming and weeping—*I hate this, I won't, I won't*—and the other women in their woolen dresses and thick stockings and sweaters buttoned high tried to crowd around her. *You'll catch a cold*, one of them said, *come back inside*. The young woman, barefoot, tried to escape the hands of the women but she could not. *It's the worst thing that can happen to a person*, she said, *the very worst thing!* But the women around her said, *Nonsense* and *Calm yourself* and *Dear, my dear, please come back inside now, please come back inside*. And eventually she did, still weeping, retreat into the store.

I thought of telling Mr. Kercher this story but I didn't know if I had seen or imagined or dreamed it. No, there was no use in saying it. I set that image back down in me.

I wouldn't have come to this place if my daughter hadn't been here, Mr. Kercher said, *but I've found a way to make a life here that is acceptable. These woods are here. There is a lake a short drive away, also. I go there. Much of the day, I am reading books.*

Mr. Kercher began to cry without making a sound, but after a moment he seemed to fold up this cry and put it away like a handkerchief. He smiled with soft confusion at the ground.

For many years I have tried, but it is difficult for me to make peace with her joining the Hindmans' church—though of course she would. She married him. But she was never religious before. In school she studied philosophy and came home for the holidays each year just—bursting. She wanted to talk about everything, reason through everything. She would have me read all the books she had in this class or that one. She shared all her papers. She was always carving away at this thing that belonged to her—her way of thinking, her beliefs . . . Ava.

Then—I don't know exactly when . . . maybe it wasn't until she'd been at this church here for some time or perhaps it happened sooner and I didn't realize—the Ava who wanted to know everything was gone. She stopped reading like she had. We didn't speak about it, and I didn't want to challenge her new life. She'd chosen this young man, moved here for him, joined this church, began having the children, doing all the work at home to take care of them . . . Of course I respect that. She was our only child, so it was somewhat natural for her to want to have many children of her own—perhaps to correct the mistakes she saw her parents making, the solitude of her childhood. And perhaps, I've thought, this is a way for her to be with her mother again, to become a mother in order to remember her mother . . .

One of her daughters looks so much like my late wife that it's . . . startling. I know my granddaughters are all their own people, of course—people don't repeat—but it's natural to go looking for the dead in new faces. But what about when you lose someone who is still alive? When you lose track of the person you know within a person they've become—what kind of grief is that?

I shook my head. Mr. Kercher shook his, too.

It has only been recently that I started to ask Ava about the questions she used to debate so tirelessly with me, and we hardly ever agreed about everything—in fact it seems we never completely agreed about anything. She was the one who claimed atheism, which led me to put forth the idea, perhaps, that some mysteries in nature made me wonder if there was some sort of . . . larger consciousness . . . something beyond human consciousness . . . well, she would become so impassioned in rebutting this idea. Reason, reason, reason, she'd say. She had no patience, she said, for the waffling agnostics or those *blindly seduced by deism. Her words! I won't repeat them to her now . . .*

*Recently she said to me—she said—*God spoke to me, and now I don't question it. *That put an end to our discussion . . . she put an end to it. She didn't want to be questioned. When someone says they heard something you did not hear, and they know you did not hear it, then you cannot tell them they did not hear what they believe they heard. They have heard their desire to hear something, and desire always speaks the loudest. It is the loudest and most confounding emotion—wanting.*

Mr. Kercher's voice disappeared into the pines, the creek, the soil and stones. His hands were palm up on each knee and his face tilted up. His mouth hung slack awhile, then shut.

It's always seemed to me—and as I get older, I feel this even more intensely—that kindness to other people comes with its own reward. It can be immediately felt. And the only thing I can see that a belief in divinity makes possible in this world is a right toward cruelty—the belief in an afterlife being the real life . . . not here. People need a sense of righteousness to take things from others . . . to carry out violence. Divinity gives them that. It creates the reins for cruelty . . .

Mr. Kercher stood up then and looked around him, as if he'd just remembered where he was. All his crying was gone then. *I'm so sorry to take up all this time.* He smiled and looked around as if suddenly lost. *I don't usually say so much.* He put his hands in his pockets and removed them. *There's really so little to say.*

HILDA WAS ON THE PORCH when Mr. Kercher and I approached. The air was already heavy. Somewhere in the neighborhood, a lawn mower purred.

I wish there was something else I could do, he said. *I wish there was anything I could do to help.* He shook his head a little, but I wasn't sure why.

Did you have a nice little walk? Hilda asked.

She squinted across the street, waved her whole arm at Mr. Kercher, who was looking back toward us.

Thank you, Mr. Kercher! she shouted. *Have a good day now, you hear?*

Yes. And you.

Will I see you at Butch and Kitty's later on?

Mr. Kercher stood still a moment, looked to his feet. *I don't believe so.*

All right, well, you have a good day now. Hilda's voice was loud and firm, a stone.

Yes.

IN THE DAYLIGHT that large house looked even larger, like a courthouse. Several cars and trucks were parked on both sides of the street. We walked beside the house, passed through a side gate, down a stone-paved path, past one of those trees that tried to grasp the sky, past flowers gasping in the heat.

Hilda knocked on a glass door and Kitty came to let us in. Inside, the house was thick with voices and noise. Kitty spoke to Hilda awhile, then turned to me—

Now I wish Nelson could be here to keep you company but he's in school and I couldn't get him out of school without upsetting the other kids—you know, we try not to favor him over the others or give him anything different or special. We try to treat them all equal.

I was given a glass of ice tea and a little chair in the corner of the kitchen. Several women were moving things in and out of ovens, arranging things on wide platters, slicing things with knives. The one that had spoken to me last time was there, too, her white apron stiff and clean, and her dark hair still pulled back tight, as if nothing at all had happened or changed since I'd last seen her. She fled the kitchen through swinging doors and I heard a wave of voices come toward us from the next room.

Why does this feel so much like a funeral? I heard one of the women ask another.

I know what you mean. People are in that mood. I guess it's just . . . well, people do sort of get like that right before the festival, don't they?

Jimmie Lee's car got broken into last night and someone stole the Karlton children's bikes right out of their garage this week, a woman said as she layered ham on a platter.

Is that so? Hilda asked.

Four whole bicycles. I keep forgetting the festival's Saturday, the woman said, speaking as if to that platter of meat.

Across the kitchen a child in a clean pink dress and white bow was busying herself in a toy kitchen—moving things into and out of the little oven, arranging plastic foods on plastic platters. A small television in the other corner spoke muffled words to the room.

Sometimes, Kitty said, loudly enough to address the entire room, *I feel like—if I just keep that television on all day, then nothing bad can happen, you know what I mean? Like a watched pot, like that kind of thing. Then other times it's almost the other way around—like I know something is going to go wrong eventually and I don't want to be the last to know.*

I know what you mean, one woman said, and others nodded and said, yes, they also knew what she meant.

Did y'all hear about what those couple of old ladies over at the Glendale Retirement Home said about Pew? one woman asked the rest of them. *They think he's an archangel. Ain't that something?*

The room grew busy with their voices—*Ain't that some-*

thing—I thought Pew was a she—Shh—They're even taking bets about it—

Well, couldn't it be! one of the women said as she carved slices of bright pink meat. *Happened in the Bible. Happened in the Bible all the time.*

Well. Kitty cleared her throat and exchanged a look with another woman who raised her eyebrows and pinched her mouth in a strange smile. *I suppose that is true.* Kitty's back was still turned to the woman with the ham.

The voices coming from the other room had quieted a little and for a moment I could hear the oven groan with heat. The woman with the ham was looking at me the way a mechanic looks down at an engine, quietly laying down years of knowledge.

Well, ain't this so much fun? Kitty said. *I don't hardly ever get into this kitchen anymore, but I ought to just fire my girl and invite all of y'all over every night—how about that?*

A small crash came from the other side of the room. The child at the tiny kitchen was lying on the floor, grinning, surrounded by a splay of wooden blocks.

Jill! You've wrinkled up your dress, honey. Kitty rushed to the child and lifted her to her feet. *And we've got company. Darlin', the whole church is practically here and we don't have time to iron it back out, so everyone is going to see you in a wrinkled dress.*

The whole church? Jill asked.

What do we do when company's over? What did I tell you?

Act nice.

That's right, honey, and what else?

Look nice.

And is a wrinkled-up dress nice?

Jill swayed, looked at the floor with a vague sadness.

Is it nice, honey?

No, the child said, soft as a bird speaking on the other side of a window.

And now you have to wear a wrinkled dress in front of everyone. Now how does that suit you?

Jill looked toward me as if looking through a glass dome.

WHEN I WAS BROUGHT into the other room, voices halted and throats cleared. I kept my eyes down, but felt the gaze of some eyes and the reluctant stare of others.

Three couches and a few armchairs had been pushed against the sides of the room and the center was filled with folding chairs, most of which held people with little plates of food in their laps and hands.

A woman with a great pile of hair gave me a crowded plate—two slices of pie, a thick sandwich, a mess of fruits—then pointed me toward a chair beside a large potted fern. I sat there. Across the room a man carefully chewed the roasted leg of what was once a bird.

Kitty stood at the front of the room clanging an empty wineglass with a knife.

I want to thank you all for coming all sudden like this. Now I know the idea for a meeting was a little, well—there has been some disagreement about what to do about the situation—but I want to thank you all for believing in us, for making it possible for us to take action as a community. To start us out, Harold Grimshaw is going to say a few words.

A short man wearing a pale gray suit stood up, his hands gathered in a large fist just held to his chest.

Now, I think I know pretty much everyone in the room, but for those of you I haven't had the pleasure to get to know yet, my name is Harold H. Grimshaw the fifth. My father was Harold H. Grimshaw the fourth and my grandfather was Harold H. Grimshaw the third and my great-grandfather was Harold H. Grimshaw the second and we were all named after my great-great-grandfather Harold H. Grimshaw, and he was one of the people who founded this town, brought the railway here, was mayor for a time, did all sorts of good for our community, and my family—the Grimshaws—we still believe in this community—as we've always believed in this community—and we work hard to serve our community every day, all of us.

Harold began to pace in the little area he had at the front of the room.

And me in particular—well, anyone can know anything about me—I've got nothing to hide. I can tell you where I went to college, what I studied, where I've traveled. I can tell you the first time I laid my eyes on Birdie Lee and I can tell you the story of how I proposed to her and the day she became my wife. I can tell you about our children. I could tell you with certainty that I've been on the fifth pew back on the west side of the sanctuary every Sunday except for days I was sick and the days my children were born—all of them on Sundays, and ain't that something?

Amen, a voice in the crowd shouted.

And I would show anyone my calendars, tell you whom I met with on which days, which cases I've worked on and how I've spent every day of my life. And I would—I would happily share any of this information with anyone in our community who wanted it. This is all because I love this town and I trust you all and I don't have anything to hide.

133

A large man in the back of the room said, *Attaboy, Harry!*
Everyone in the room applauded, some whistling, some clapping, and at once it felt like a real place, a real thing, this room, this feeling in this room. Everyone knew everyone and they all belonged to one another. There was a certainty, a clarity, a real joy, that fused them all into one, into one massive entity, the weight of their years all pressed together, thousands of years in the room, all together like that, entwined with one another, no distance between any of them, no loneliness, no solitude—and it was easy to see, just then, how intensely one could want to belong here.

And since I really trust and respect my community, I'm willing to share anything with them. I like to think my community is worthy of trust and care, and though, of course, I do try to take heed of the least of those—care for those who have no one, those who are lost—I know that I have to first protect my community, my children, my family, above all else, which is my duty as a father and man of this community. But we have to hold everyone to the same standard, don't we? Treating everybody equal. Be fair.

And so, we have a problem on our hands with the recent arrival of our new friend. You may already know that Pew, who hasn't spoken a word since being found, got their nickname because they illegally broke into a church to have a night's sleep. And what did we make of this, friends?

A few people shifted in their creaking folding chairs. Someone dropped a plate of food and there was a hushed scuffle to clean it up.

What did we make of this? Harold asked. No one answered. I could hear jaws chewing crackers and people putting soft little cakes in their mouths. *We ask Pew where they've come from—nothing. What he needs—nothing. What happened to him—or her. Quite frankly we still don't know if Pew is a boy or girl, we don't know Pew's age, we don't know Pew's real name, or if anyone out there might be missing Pew—and even if we ask any of these things, we get nothing. And there's not even any agreement about Pew's heritage, his nationality, her race—everyone's in disagreement about where Pew might be* from *and it's troubling, ain't it? I, for one, have never seen nobody that looks quite like our guest here—*

Someone at the back of the room stood up to say, *Harry, this isn't what we agreed upon, this isn't the way you said you'd—*

Hold on now, I'm getting to it, Harold said.

Hilda crept up beside Harold and whispered something into his ear.

All right—all right, I've been told to stick to the script! Our women sure do keep us in line, don't they? Everyone laughed. The whole room laughed. Even the furniture and floor seemed to be laughing.

All I'm trying to say is that the timing is peculiar, ain't it? And we are all a little on edge because of the situation in Almose and I think we should be on edge, that is, we should have our eyes out here for anything . . . unusual. And it's rather unusual to be silent, ain't it? To refuse to speak. After all, I sure like to talk. Everyone I know likes to talk. We all talk together, don't we? We all discuss things out loud, as that is the way our culture has taught us, isn't it now? Storytelling. Sharing. Of course, I don't want to jump to any conclusions. And I'm certainly not jumping to any conclusions. I have my hunches, of course, but then we have the judicial process for a reason, don't we? We don't want to stoop to the level of trying this person in the court of public opinion, now do we? There's a due process. So what I figure the next logical step is, is for us to consider the reasons a person might go silent—

Harold, Kitty said from the side of the room, waving her hand a little, *can we just go back to what we planned—*

For instance, in the news recently you may have heard about how a little girl showed up down in Greenville, and she couldn't seem to speak but the police figured that probably what happened was—well, the same thing that makes a lot of little girls go quiet for a while, which is that someone must have roughed her up a bit and she's just scared is all. It happens. Things happen. But everyone in Greenville that saw this girl could agree that she was a girl of about seven years old and she was very obviously American, white, and they easily found the documents for her—birth certificate, fingerprints from her Girl Scouts—I think most importantly, her silence, her being mute—it didn't cause anyone any trouble because—I think—it was obvious that she *wasn't trying to* cause *trouble. She wasn't trying to hide anything because she didn't have anything to hide, and they took her to a hospital and let her settle down for a while and after a few days she did end up telling the authorities what she remembered, what happened to her—an awful story, I don't need to go over it here. But she's doing all right now, recovering. And you know why? Because she's talking. Because she wanted to get better.*

I looked at the plate in my hands. The pie bled dark syrup into the sandwich bread.

You know, it's stories like that—and I have to read a lot of them being a lawyer and all—it's stories like that one that can really depress you if you let them, but I always remind myself they are outliers. And like everyone in this room, I want justice to prevail, for the good side to win. And in order for that to happen we have got to know who people are. *Who they* really are.

It's what makes us civilized—we can identify ourselves and we can identify each other! That's how we keep track of things, hold people accountable. That's how we know who we're related to and who's related to us. That's how we know who is our wife and who is our neighbor's wife . . . so that, well . . .

Laughter burst in the room, a pressure released.

Sorry, Birdie Lee! Harold shouted.

They laughed like a herd of something running.

It's good to hear us laughing together again, ain't it?

Harold looked around the room and nodded. I could feel people nodding with him, then the laughter gave way to applause, and the air in the room—human, humid—churned around me.

OK! Thank you, Harold, Kitty said, chiming her wineglass with a knife again. *Now, at this point, we're going to hear from a few others about their experiences with Pew and their ideas about how we should move forward. Now I think Hilda Bonner was going to speak a little. Hilda?*

Yes. Hilda stood, smoothed out her dress and touched her hair, and turned toward the room, her hands clasping each other in a fist over her chest.

Now speak up, Hilda, my dear, Harold shouted.

Yes, it's just that, I wasn't—I didn't know that . . . Hilda leaned over to whisper something into the ear of Kitty, who nodded to her.

All right, Hilda said. *Well. Thank you all for coming out this afternoon. It's just so nice to see all your faces. And thank you to Kitty and Butch for hosting us in their beautiful home. And to all the ladies who helped put the refreshments together.*

A breeze of claps swept through. Hilda nodded and looked around and smiled, then looked at me, her smile bending a little.

So I was just going to tell everyone what happened, though Harold said a little of it—anyway, I just wanted to tell you what happened on Sunday, so everyone has their stories straight and we can figure out what to do.

When we got to our pew on Sunday, we found this young person sleeping there and I didn't know what to do—honestly, it fright-ened me a little, the situation did, but Steven was calm about it—

A good man, your husband, Steven Bonner, Harold said, *a very good man.*

Thank you. So—Steven thought we should just sit there as usual and wait for Pew to wake up and then we'd take them out for lunch with the boys. So we did that, and Steven and I decided that we could let, um, Pew stay at our house for a little while, because our son Jack—

An extraordinary young man, Harold said. *I had him in Scouts three years in a row and he is truly a fine, strong young man.*

Thank you. Well—Jack had been setting up his own room in the attic, so we moved him back down to his brothers' room and let Pew stay up there. The Reverend, he came over for supper that night and he was the one who came up with Pew's name. Well . . . our boys took Pew in like another member of the family, they really did. Which made it sad when my husband caught Pew trying to sneak out one night. After all that we were trying to do and everything.

I'll admit that I was suspicious after that, and, well, it was the next day that Pew refused to be examined at Monroe Medical—

Yes, tell us about what happened at Monroe, Harold said.

Well, I drove Pew out there early on Wednesday morning, but when they told Pew it was time to do the examination, well, each time they came back to the room to start the examination, Pew hadn't put on the paper gown like the doctor had asked.

So, Harold interrupted, *you drove Pew all the way out to Monroe Medical and an examination didn't even happen?*

That's right.

And it didn't happen because Pew wouldn't undress?

Yes, that's right.

And what was it that made you think that Pew needed to be examined?

Well, for one, we just wanted to make sure Pew was healthy. *We don't know where she—or he—had been, you know, or whether . . . or whether their nutrition had been all right, things like that. Mainly we wanted to do that for Pew's sake, of course, because who knows how long it had been since Pew had been to a doctor. And also we wanted to make sure Pew didn't have anything that might be . . . contagious or something.*

Like taking a stray in to the vet, Harold said, *to get their shots.*

Oh, I suppose so, Hilda said. *I hadn't thought of it exactly like that, but I guess so.*

In the middle of the room Dr. Winslow stood up and Hilda shut her mouth.

Buddy, Harold said, *would you like to say something?*

Yes, well, I'd just like to clear up one little item here. Part of the reason we couldn't complete the examination—that is, in addi-

tion to Pew's refusal to cooperate—was that we were incredibly short-staffed, and all of the equipment we use for an uncooperative patient was in use elsewhere in the facility. It was a particularly busy morning—as is usually the case the week before the festival as people tend to have more heart attacks and accidents and such around this time of year—but we're also badly in need of some new equipment and supplies, and our budget requests have gone unanswered for so long that Betty has been thinking about doing a fund-raiser—maybe a cakewalk or a raffle. I'd just like to point out that otherwise our success rate at Monroe Medical is really tremendous—and I'm proud of my whole team of nurses, remarkable girls—so I don't want anyone to get the wrong idea about us. We do very good work.

Excellent, yes, Harold said.

Absolutely the best work, the best rehabilitation and trauma care in the whole state, probably the whole country, Hilda said.

A few people began to applaud, then everyone joined, cheering and clapping until they seemed to grow tired.

Speaking of fund-raisers, now, that's an idea, ain't it? That we could do some kind of fund-raiser for Pew to get the right services or help?

Oh, that's a good one, Kitty said.

I have an idea, a person in the front row said. *Why can't we have Dr. Winslow try to do an examination again? It seems to me that it's an issue of the security and safety of our community—ain't it?*

A small voice came from the back of the room, somewhere within the crowd, from a face I couldn't see. *But what if—if*

Pew, that is, what if Pew won't get undressed again? I'm just very concerned . . .

The voice went soft and pale.

All right now, Harold shouted, *just speak up if you will.*

Well, the pale voice said, *I'm just concerned that . . . well . . . It seems like Pew should have the right to—*

Well, of course no one likes going to the doctor, a louder voice shouted. *But we all have to go from time to time. We all have to cooperate, you know.*

That's not quite what I mean, the pale voice said. *I just think, well, I don't want Pew to be in a situation where someone is forcing them—against their will. It makes me uncomfortable to think—*

Yes, Harold said, *I think we all understand that there are a lot of things about this whole situation that make people uncomfortable. And that's why we're having this meeting. To decide, as a community, how to proceed with the maximum amount of people comfortable with what is going on.*

It's all a bunch of horseshit, someone said. *Excuse me, but I'm the only one old enough to say it like it is, to spell it out—but we all know it's true. It's horseshit. This is about public health! And we all know what you're* implying *and we all know it's horseshit.*

Strong opinions there. Harold stood again and took a kind of control of the room. *But let's table that one for now and move on to other concerns. Do we have any other concerns at the moment?*

Kitty raised her hand.

Mrs. Goodson, do you have an idea?

She stood, taking her time, comfortable in the gaze of her guests.

Now, as I understand it, Pew did some drawings with Roger Smith that might be revealing about where Pew came from and what we can do to help Pew. I know that his work with my adopted son, Nelson, who is a childhood refugee and orphan of a horrific war—well, his work with Nelson was very helpful. Maybe we can have some experts analyze the drawings that Pew made with Roger.

A fine idea, Mrs. Goodson, Harold said. *Hilda, make sure you write that one down. And, Kitty, I would just like to say that we're all very moved by you taking that poor child into your home. Could there be anything more Christian than that?*

Everyone in the room applauded, and as they applauded, Mrs. Goodson turned to smile at each person in the room, waving at everyone with one hand, then the other.

A woman with raised eyebrows stood. *I have something I'd like to tell the group.*

Go on, Mrs. Robertson, Harold said.

Now I was just sitting here talking to Minnie Sims about Pew and I must tell y'all, we have some real disagreements about what . . . Pew looks like. I mean, to me, it's so obviously a girl and definitely not white, I'd say about thirteen or fourteen years old, but Minnie, she is convinced that Pew's a boy and white and at least fifteen!

More white than not white is what I said, Minnie clarified.

But you can see how drastic our difference of opinion is, the standing woman said, her eyebrows arched high on her forehead. *It's almost like we're looking at two different people! And I don't feel comfortable letting Pew be around other teens—you know—if we don't even know if they're this way or that. Does everyone else have such different ideas about what Pew looks like?*

A burst of voices, raised hands. Harold tried to conduct them with a little knife against a glass, then with a fork against a ceramic plate, then by shouting.

A voice from the back cut through the noise—*We ought to have Pew baptized*—and the room quieted around that suggestion.

Oh, yes, Harold said. *We should take care of that this Sunday. A very important point. Thank you for bringing it up, Bill.*

No sweat, Bill said.

In the meantime, I think perhaps we'll have a short break, freshen up our plates and coffees? Everyone began to stand and their voices grew into a low rumble. *Marlena Dean made her famous pimento cheese, so don't miss that.*

There's pie on the side table in the dining room, Kitty said to the room.

Yes, there's pie, Harold repeated.

THE WOMAN IN THE WHITE APRON was washing dishes as Kitty led me into the kitchen.

Maria, if you could just keep an eye on Pew for the next—I don't know—might take an hour. Just take Pew back to the den, please, if you don't mind—the walls are thin up here and I don't want the discussion to bother, uh—to bother anyone.

In the den, yes, no problem. Maria dried her hands on a towel and came toward me, chewing at one corner of her lip.

A girl appeared at the back door's window, looked at me carefully, then opened it slowly and came inside.

Annie, what on earth!

Why are there all these cars here?

Why aren't you in school?

Are y'all meeting about the Forgiveness Festival?

It's not particularly your business what it's about, when I haven't any idea about why you're not in school.

Annie put her backpack on the floor and took a cube of cheese from a ravaged platter. Kitty held her open palm under her daughter's face—*Spit it.* Annie puckered her lips and slowly pushed out a half-gnawed cube of cheese. Maria immediately removed the waste from Kitty's hand and wiped it clean.

I clearly don't have time for this, Annie. There's company and I'm expected back in there at this very moment.

Annie looked to me, back at her mother.

You remember Pew from dinner on Monday, don't you? The Bonners' guest?

Annie looked at me again. A half smile passed over her face.

Don't be rude, Annie. Say hello.

Hello.

Maria was just taking Pew back to the den, so I want you to go immediately to your room and do your homework until I come get you, do you understand?

Fine. Annie left through one door as Maria took me through another.

I HAD BEEN SITTING on the edge of a bathtub for some time when there was a knock at the door. *Ah, Pew? You need something?* Maria's voice.

I hadn't heard her footsteps so she must have followed me, must have been sitting at the door the whole time.

Knock once to say you're OK?

A long silence.

Just let me know.

I picked up a bar of soap and threw it at the door. It fell to the tiles, dented.

OK. I'll leave you alone. Come check later. Her footsteps pattered, faded.

I lowered myself into the empty tub, felt the cool porcelain slowly warm. Elsewhere in the house there were voices overlapping, laughing, a clang in the kitchen, then a sound came closer—something just behind the wall.

A vent in the corner popped off and a thin leg appeared, then another leg, then Annie slid out onto the bathroom floor, at first looking surprised to see me, then seeming steely and defiant.

It didn't sound like anyone was in here, she whispered.

She looked at me awhile and I looked back at her. Her hair was tangled. She went to the medicine cabinet, got out a little

146

blue tube. She squeezed something thick out of it and smeared it across her face as she stared in the mirror.

Everyone's talking about you at school, she said to her reflection. *Not that you should care. They're all so stupid. Jack started it. He's such an asshole. He knew he wasn't supposed to talk about you except with people from church who already knew, but he told pretty much everybody. He's so dumb.*

She had covered half her face in a thick sky-blue paste when she stopped and examined herself more closely in the mirror.

Sometimes I think that nobody is just one person, that actually we're a bunch of different people and we have to figure out how to get them all to cooperate and fool everyone else into thinking that we're just one person, even though everybody else is doing the same thing.

She turned to me.

Well? Don't you think so, or what?

She turned back to the mirror, kept applying the pale blue paste to her face.

Mom said I would talk to a wall if I felt like it was listening. Anyway it's her dumb idea I have to put this stuff on because she caught me sneaking one of her cigarettes and got mad at me because she said it gives you premature wrinkles and gray hair. I have a gray hair—do you want to see it?

She washed the stuff from her hands and began combing her hair, staring into the mirror.

There! She came toward me, leaned over the tub, and pinched a single white hair. *See it? Mom saw one on the back of my head a couple weeks ago and she yanked it out so I have to hide this one so she doesn't get it. I like him.*

Annie sat on the tiled floor. The paste was turning pale and dry at the edges. Some of her hair clung to it.

Anyway. You're lucky they don't send you to school. I almost wanted to be mad about why they sent me home today, but I was just too glad to leave.

She leaned back onto her elbows and looked up at the ceiling.

It was in science class. She was teaching us about flower reproduction and she said that everything that was alive could reproduce, and everything that could reproduce was either male or female and I raised my hand and even though she saw me, she didn't call on me, so after a while I just interrupted her and said it wasn't true, that some things that reproduced didn't have a sex. I'd been studying about this on my own because of something I saw on TV about starfish—that a starfish reproduces all by itself without having to mate or anything. And snails. And there are plants like that, too, and some animals even switch back and forth, and I always thought that was just something that happened in science fiction but it's not just in science fiction. So I said this, I said to Mrs. Goldwater, I said, What about dandelions and how they're all asexual and reproduce all by themselves? *And Mrs. Goldwater just said,* Maybe that's why they're considered to be a weed. *But she didn't even know what she was talking about, and she just said that so the class would laugh and they did, even Jeremy, who I know is gay because he told me himself, plus everyone can tell, so I kept asking Mrs. Goldwater about the starfish and about how seahorses do it the other way around, and the boy seahorses carry the babies, and most of the class was laughing because they're so dumb and then I got sent to the principal's office.*

Annie lay fully on her back and was quiet for a while.

In the library I also found a book about revolutions that had a whole section just about people who set themselves on fire as a protest. It makes you wonder, don't it? Makes me wonder.

She got up to look at her face in the mirror. The paste had mostly dried out and turned faintly gray. She touched it.

Almost. She hoisted herself to sit on the edge of the sink and kicked her feet into the air for a while, then stilled them and looked at me.

So are they going to make you go to the festival?

I just looked at her awhile, then said, *I don't know.*

How old are you?

I sat up a little. *I don't know.*

I'm fifteen. Do you answer everything with I don't know*?*

Sometimes.

That's really Nelson's thing, you know. He hates talking.

Annie turned around and rinsed her face clean in the sink, speaking into the water as she worked. *And how come you were sleeping in that church? Was it just because you don't have a home or did you pick our church in particular? Or did you run away from somewhere?*

She stood up and dried her face with a white towel. For the first time I could almost remember where I'd come from before all the walking, before the searching every night for a place to sleep. I wanted to tell her something. I wanted to begin speaking and not know what I was going to say, but I couldn't. I couldn't speak.

You know, you don't have to talk if you don't want to. I'm not trying to make you tell me anything, you know. My dad says I ask too many questions anyway. It's just that, if you don't have a home, I think that's really . . . well, it upsets me, that's all. It makes me sad and I wish I could do something about it.

She dropped the towel onto the floor and went over to the window, peeked between the blinds she parted with two fingers.

In civics class last semester we had to write these essays about something we could do to make the world a better place. It was only supposed to be a page but I wrote seven and a half pages about how everyone should get exactly the same stuff—everyone could live in the same normal-sized houses, and there should only be public schools that everyone can go to instead of private ones that only rich people get to go to, and when people die, they shouldn't be able to give all their money to their kids. It should all get split up between the poorest people because otherwise rich people's kids start out way ahead of everyone else just because of where they were born and poor people's kids start out worse off than everyone else just because they were born somewhere else. And anyway, I had all these other ideas in there because it was seven and a half pages, typed up and everything. But guess what happened when my teacher read it? She said I had to go talk to the school counselor because I was a communist. And I told her I never said I was a communist and she had my essay and she held it up and said, Miss Goodson, this is very troubling, *and I said,* Because I want people to be treated the same, *and she said something about how ideas were dangerous and I really needed someone to talk some sense into me before it got worse and this is not how the world works and I said that I knew that wasn't how the world works but it was how I think the world* should *work, then she wrote me up for talking back. Isn't that stupid, too, getting in trouble for talking back? No offense to you because you can do whatever you want, but aren't we supposed to talk back to each other? That's like—a whole half of discussion. It just seems to me that part of some people having a lot of things depends on other people having less things. The school counselor wasn't much better and basically she made me so mad that I threw a chair across the room, which I know wasn't the right thing to do, but it ended up proving one of my points about how everyone gets treated unequally because when a guy did that last semester, he got suspended but the school counselor just laughed at me. Didn't even write me up or nothing. Which isn't fair.*

Annie leaned back into the window, and the blinds clattered.

I'm probably talking too much. They all say I talk too much. I know I shouldn't but there's so much that bothers me and everyone just keeps acting like it's normal. But it doesn't have to be normal. You probably just think this is stupid.

No, I said.

Well. You might be the only one who thinks so. I don't know how anyone can stand this place. My mom said that saying you hate your hometown is the sign of a boring person who thinks they're better than everyone else. And anyway this week is the worst of it— right before the festival. I already know about three different girls that— Well, it's the worst for girls, I think. Everyone's more worried about their houses or cars getting broken into, since everything gets forgiven at the festival and it all goes away. Anyway, most of the time the girls don't even say anything about what happens to them because then they get into trouble for it . . . and anyway they'd just tell you to pray about it at the festival anyway, that there's nothing they can do about it now . . .

We heard footsteps in the hall and Annie braced, looked toward the door.

It's locked, she whispered, *isn't it?*

I nodded.

I better go anyway. As she started to crawl back into the vent she'd come from, she turned to me again and whispered, *Pew isn't your real name, is it?*

I shook my head.

Does anyone know what your true name is?

I didn't know what to say.

Somebody does know your true name, don't they?

I just kept sitting there, breathing in and out, running my fingers along the slick sides of the bathtub. Annie began to cry a little, silently, her face crumpled up and reddened. She slapped herself hard in the face, once, then twice, then once more.

Somebody should know, she said, then she slid herself back into the vent and crawled away, replacing the slatted cover from the inside.

Bye, she said, within the wall.

Alone again I felt a prickling sort of illness. I shut my eyes, flattened my body against the bottom of the tub, tried to hide myself into nothing the way snakes do when a storm is coming. I tried to remember what a damp field smells like in the morning, in that kind of morning before the true morning, those hours before the sun has risen and the earth feels like a lung. I tried to breathe in the way the field breathes then.

Several hard knocks at the door. Harold's voice came from the other side—*Pew, my friend?*

A long pause.

It seems you've had quite enough time in the bathroom, my child. There's some people down there in the living room that would like to say goodbye to you and it's just not polite to keep them waiting so long.

I came to understand that I was not a field. I was not, to-day, just dirt and seed and grass. A field is a living thing. Fields began and ended. Every plant has a true name that no one had to give them. People were the end of something. The body is already dead.

If I need to, Harold said through laughter, *I can pick the lock, but I don't need to do that, now, do I?*

People cannot be kept waiting. Sometimes one of us will hold the other by the neck. Sometimes one of us will hold the other by the neck and no one will do anything about it for many years, so many lifetimes of necks being held. I know what I am. The body is already dead.

Wouldn't you like to walk out on your own accord?

All breath is taken and given through the throat. All air is borrowed. People cannot be kept waiting.

HILDA DROVE IN SILENCE. Whatever had made it possible for her to look into my eyes, it seemed, had now expired. There would be no more of that. She cleared her throat several times, trying and failing to fully clear it. I stared out the window and saw, every mile or so, a plain white sign with red type. The first one was beside a large, gnarled tree—

> THE FESTIVAL
> SAVES.

And sometime later—

> FORGIVENESS:
> FOR OR AGAINST?

And the last one, stuck crookedly in the grass of a highway median—

> THE
> FORGIVENESS FESTIVAL:
> SOUL HEALER!

Harold—well, he's very prominent. People respect him and when he gets going on something, well, he can be a little overactive. That's all.

By the time we had arrived at her house, she had submerged into silence again. On the front porch a potted plant had somehow been knocked over.

Oh, Hilda said as she passed.

The plant was trying to grow toward the sun again, bending, trying. Soil spilled out through the cracked ceramic. Dark afternoon clouds crept into the sky, turned the house ghostly and gray. I could hear two different clocks ticking, each to its own count.

Hilda opened the door to the attic, and as I climbed the stairs, she said I was free to come down whenever I wanted, but that she and Steven had agreed that the attic door would be kept locked just to be safe and should I need to come downstairs I should just knock on the door as loudly as I could and she would come let me out and sit with me in the living room or the porch or wherever I would like to be. Her focus fell from me to the floor, to a wall, to a stair, to the door, to the knob in her hand, to the floor, briefly to me again, to a wall.

I knew I would not leave the attic. I nodded.

And it's not that we think you've done anything wrong—it's just that we don't know what you've done. We just want to be careful.

She stood there quietly awhile, no longer breathing from the top of her lungs and no longer letting her focus drift from one place to another; it seemed she wasn't breathing at all, that she wasn't looking at anything.

I SAT BESIDE the attic window, waiting for night to come, for the light to leave us and for the fireflies to appear. It was somehow more important than ever that I see the fireflies hovering in the yard, the way they flashed and vanished and reappeared and vanished—that they could be and not be, be again and again not be.

Below me I heard Hilda call out across the house to Steven, heard Steven shout back, their voices muffled, urgent. I stayed still at my place beside the window, sat there looking out at the night. A firefly appeared and I touched the warm glass.

The door to the attic opened and Hilda's voice echoed in the stairwell—*Pew? Could you come downstairs a minute, please?*

Several lamps glowed behind shades in the living room. The parrot inched across his caged perch. The room was still and quiet enough to hear his talons grip and ungrip.

We want you to know what's going on, Steven said. *All the decisions that have been made so far.*

Yes, Hilda said, then we all sat silent again awhile. *We thought it was important that you know.*

The boys are staying over at their grandmother's house tonight, Steven said. *After today's meeting, I talked with a few people from the community and they all agreed that it wasn't a good idea to keep you so close to the boys. People had lots of different reasons for this and I have my own reasons, not that we need to get into them—*

We don't need to get into them, Hilda said, though Steven spoke over her.

—because they're not really for you to know. It's just a decision I've made about my family and it's ultimately a private decision, a family decision. What I will say is that Jack's behavior both at home and at school this week was very unusual for him.

He's usually not so— Hilda stopped herself from continuing.

And I got the sense he may have been impolite to you—I didn't see it directly, but that's the sense I got—and I wanted to apologize for him. He's really not that kind of young man and he's been raised right, but he even got a detention this week at school, and that's not like him, that's not our Jack. He's always loved going to church, the music, the morality of it . . . It just seems with everything going on, he's been set off is all.

I hadn't come here, I knew then. I had always been here, and I knew I had always been here but I didn't say that. I hadn't needed even to be born here because I had always been here; I hadn't needed to be born at all. I didn't say that either. I didn't say anything.

My, it is warm, isn't it? Hilda stood. *Don't you think I should turn the air conditioner up a little? Seems the summer just won't quit. I keep thinking, tomorrow it'll be cool, that it will finally cool off, but it keeps not happening.*

She was talking to herself as she left the room, but I couldn't make out the words.

The other thing I was told to discuss with you is that you're going to be staying with the Corbin family, I believe, at least tomorrow night, maybe longer, we don't know yet. Dr. Corbin is going to come get you in the morning.

Hilda had returned but stayed close to the door, fanning herself with her hands. She wiped sweat from her forehead.

He's the reverend at Second Baptist, on the other side of town, which is, well, I suppose to put it bluntly it's the black side of town, if that's all right to say—is that all right to say, Hilda?

I—I think so, Hilda said.

Some people at the meeting today thought maybe you'd be more comfortable with them, that maybe you'd talk to those people if you won't talk to us. Or maybe you'd rather live with someone over there if you don't like living with us. Personally, I don't know exactly why they decided for it to go this way, and I just don't see why it should make any difference, but this is what I was told to tell you. I suppose there's some disagreement about . . . well, I suppose some people think you look like one thing and some people think you look like something else and it seems you won't speak up and break the tie so we're just doing what we can. Now, I don't mean for that to sound ugly, and I ain't trying to be ugly to you. No one here is trying to be ugly, but we just—we never had this sort of issue before. Some people find it a little frustrating is all. But Dr. Corbin, from what I understand, is a very respected man, so you'll stay over there for at least one night and they'll bring you to the festival.

Hilda leaned down to whisper something in Steven's ear.

Well, I thought they were going to be the ones to explain it, he said.

It's just that Harold thought you might do a better job explaining, Hilda said, *since they don't even go to it anymore.*

Steven squinted for a moment, then began—

The Forgiveness Festival—well, there's a very long story about how it came to be and I'm afraid I'm not the right person to tell all the history about it, but what I can say is that the festival is what sets our community apart from other communities in the area. It's one of the ways we've decided to actively reconcile with our past, unite both sides of our community, and acknowledge that everyone—every single one of us—everyone is born broken. That's what we believe—you know—that's a core part of Christianity. That we're all broken without God. And a few years back all the preachers in town got together for a meeting because it was starting to feel like the whole country was particularly angry, and people were always accusing each other, and whole groups of people start blaming whole other groups of people for their problems—blacks and immigrants, for instance, and women, of course—but I'll admit that, in some ways, it goes the other direction, too, I suppose. Everybody really blames everybody and never blames themselves. Well, our preachers decided this had gone on long enough, so they prayed about it and they read the Bible about it—and a peculiar thing happened, which is that God spoke to all our preachers, all at once—

Hilda muttered something to herself, but Steven didn't notice and kept talking.

And what He told them was to have a special day every year for everyone to confess all their sins together—out loud—so that we all understand that we're all sinful, we're all broken, and there's no use in blaming anyone else for anyone's trouble. Of course, people still want their privacy so there's blindfolds and curtains that are set up—

It's very beautiful, Hilda said. *Even with the blindfolds. You feel how beautiful it is.*

Yes, Steven said. *And it's moving to see the community come together.*

Well, almost.

They've always been invited. We invite them every year. And Dr. Corbin, he was part of the group that put it all together anyway, but even he couldn't convince his own church to come. That's what I was told anyway.

Well. I mean. I can understand why. It's just that—

Anyway, that's neither here nor there, Steven said. *Point is, Dr. Corbin is going to bring you to the festival on Saturday so you can see for yourself what it is, and what our most important values are.*

Right.

And there are some things you might see at the festival or on the way that we decided it would be better for you to know about ahead of time.

So it doesn't startle you, Hilda said.

On the way to the festival you may see a lot of policemen in the streets.

The guns are symbolic. Hilda seemed to recite it from somewhere. *They're symbolic of the power of God, and of the powerful gifts he's given to us.*

And also, they're there just to make sure that no one gets hurt.

That's right.

Because pretty much half the town goes to the festival, so half the homes are unattended, so we have our police officers keep the neighborhoods safe, you know.

Hilda nodded, solemn.

After the festival, the community is really exceptionally safe, but we do see a few problems that happen just before—

Hilda whispered something in Steven's ear.

Oh, the rumor. Right. One thing everyone wanted to make sure was clear to you is that there's nothing to be afraid of, and I don't know what Nelson or another kid may have repeated to you—but Kitty and Butch were concerned he may have told you the rumor that has been going around the high school, something about a human sacrifice that happens at the festival, which is just some lie somebody made up to scare the younger kids—

We ease the children into it.

That's right. Most children aren't let inside for the confession part of the festival—there's a room just outside the main room where they're kept. So I think what happened is that some older kids were just trying to frighten the younger ones.

That's right, Hilda said.

Nothing to be afraid of.

Oh, no, nothing like that.

Ritual is something that's very important to us, Steven said.

Yes.

So. That's really all, I think. Dr. Corbin will drive you over and you might see more policemen on the street, and when you're inside the festival, you'll get a blindfold just like everyone else, and after that I think it will actually make a lot of sense.

Oh, yes. I think so, too. Hilda's body remained very still. It seemed she was not, for a few moments, breathing.

FRIDAY

WOKE UP HUNGRY; listened to wind whining in the trees beyond the windows. I slid out of bed, pressed my ear to the floor, heard nothing. My stomach moaned to itself and it sounded like a song.

Hilda shouted through the door, up the stairs—*Pew?*—the sound of the door unlocking—*Are you up yet?* I sat up, went to the top of the stairs. She was wearing a white robe and had her hair pulled up in a towel.

I just about forgot you were still up there, quiet as you are. Come have some grits when you're ready.

I ate standing up, facing away from her and listening to the parrot singing the same five notes over and over in the other room and after some time I looked down at an empty bowl. I put the bowl in the sink. The bird was still singing, singing as if it were practicing for something, as if this song would someday be necessary.

Dr. Corbin will be over in a couple hours. He's going to take you to lunch, I was told, then to a little party, some kind of gathering or something happening over in his neighborhood. Now you'll have to excuse me to fix my hair.

In the front room Steven was sitting in a plush chair, a newspaper shielding his head, his chest.

I sat in a chair beside the window and looked out at the thick green bush just outside. A beetle was crawling across some leaves, trying to get through them, trying to go somewhere. The morning passed like this, Steven's newspaper cracking open and closed—beetles crawling across leaves.

Dr. Corbin came in a pale beige truck with one soft, undivided seat in the front. He wore a plain gray suit. His shoulders stooped and his chest caved as if he were forever peering over the edge of something. I had the feeling he'd just realized something dear and lost to him was never coming back. He held a complicated privacy, his own slow wind.

I don't know how it is I can sometimes see all these things in people—see these silent things in people—and though it has been helpful, I think, at times, so often it feels like an affliction, to see through those masks meant to protect a person's wants and unmet needs. People wear those masks for a reason, like river dams and jar lids have a reason.

Dr. Corbin did not tell me where we were going, and I did not need to know. The truck's engine shook and muttered. I wondered if I might ever return to Hal and Tammy's house. I imagined Tammy might give me a peacock feather, something useless and beautiful, a real thing to pass between two people since we cannot see all the unphysical things that pass between people.

When the truck finally stopped, we were beside a narrow church on the edge of a field. It had been built of wood and painted white. We went inside the church, where an organ rumbled and spun, wide circles of notes sprinting around one another, frantic, unyielding. We sat in a pew in the back of the sanctuary. I could see someone's small body at the jaw of the organ, thrashing and heaving itself at the keys. The organ spoke the notes it had been built and tuned and kept here to say. An organ is a machine, I remembered, that can always cry louder than a human will.

Dr. Corbin turned to speak to me but I could not hear him through the music. His mouth moved and I watched his mouth move, and when it stopped moving, I nodded without thinking—whatever it was, I had agreed with it. We listened to the organ wail. Some time passed this way. It began to seem possible that a person might have pains and thoughts that resisted language and had to be transfigured through an instrument, turned into pure sound, spun into the air, and heard.

The organ stopped one song and began another. Another ended, another began. I began to both remember and lose the shape of the years that had led me here. I could remember a low, windowless room. Three paces by two paces. A damp floor. The taste of blood. A child. A long hunger. Some years. Some years, but gone now. They had ended and would never return and would never end. They were mine, or had been mine, but now they were somewhere else, somewhere near and far from me. They didn't belong to anyone, those untouchable years. All that was left of them was their imprint, the empty field they'd left in me.

The organist flung one arm out to turn a page of music, but all the sheets went flying, scattered in the air. The music ceased, not even a shadow of it left, and the papers fluttered and fell the way dead leaves do. A soft curse from the pulpit. The organist crouched and began to collect the scatter.

Dr. Corbin put a hand on my shoulder and smiled. We stood and left.

THE TRUCK TOOK US farther down this road until we came to a low little building with a little sign outside it, burned-out neon—DINER. When we went inside, a chime sang at the door, but no one turned to look at us. Someone wearing dirt-flecked overalls sat hunched at a counter, pushing a sandwich into their mouth. Two small people in pale orange dresses sat in a booth across from each other, one of them forking into a slice of pie and the other staring into a coffee. No music was playing. The wide windows were faintly smudged with grease.

A voice came from the kitchen—*Two plates?*

Yes, ma'am.

Someone who'd been leaning against a broom handle looked up and nodded to Dr. Corbin, who took off his hat, held it with two hands, and walked with me to the back corner. We sat in a booth and over his shoulder I could see a small television screen by the front counter—a silent, cheering crowd, their mouths stretched wide, so many trembling throats, waving flags and banners, fists punched into the air. I watched the crowd that seemed to watch me.

Nice place here. Nice vegetables, and every day different ones. Nancy is there in the kitchen. She makes a good corn bread. Makes it every day so you never have to miss it.

The chimes at the door sang again as a woman in a brightly

patterned dress came in. She glanced around the room, then paused as if startled by the sight of us.

Judy, Dr. Corbin said, as she approached our table. She looked at me, at him, then me again.

Mrs. Columbus, she corrected him, her eyes turning bright and bitter. It seemed she was using a lot of energy to just stand there above us. Her hands fidgeted with the handle of a yellow purse.

Well, Dr. Corbin said, *didn't I tell you true?*

May I sit down?

Please, Dr. Corbin said, but Mrs. Columbus kept standing. *You can see now for yourself, can't you? Are you satisfied?*

Dr. Corbin, is there something of which I am unaware that gives you permission to use such a tone with me?

Now, Judy, I just—

You may call me Mrs. Columbus.

Her every word was a stone. She was still staring at me.

Mrs. Columbus, I'm sorry. I apologize, I really do. It's just old habit. We all look for you down at the church on Sunday, but you're never there. We look every Sunday, Mrs. Columbus, and we're always ready to welcome you back. I've always—

I was told I would have some time with the child.

But you can see for yourself, can't you? Dr. Corbin pleaded. *This isn't—*

That's what I was told I'd get. That was the arrangement.

She closed her eyes and lowered her head. She was not praying. I don't know how I knew this, but I knew she was not praying. For a few long moments she was quiet in that way that requires you to listen to it. A large truck went by outside, whipping the tree branches with wind, then a pipe sighed somewhere in the wall beside me, and the cash register opened and shut at the front of the room and all our blood kept going along within us, keeping time.

Well, Dr. Corbin said. *I suppose you can have a moment here.* He stood and left us, went outside, climbed into the truck, and watched us through the scummy windows. Mrs. Columbus took his place in the booth. She looked at me as if she had known me from somewhere, but couldn't quite remember. Perhaps she did. Perhaps she still does.

I imagine you must be right tired of people trying to tell you things. I only say so because I know a thing or two about people trying to tell you something when they don't have any clue about what you need . . . It's enough to drive you half-crazy.

She set her yellow purse on the table between us.

It's been just about a year since my son Johnny went somewhere, that or got taken. I still don't know—no one seems to know. He was very close to Dr. Corbin, Johnny was. Took everything he said as gospel, you know. And I thought for a long while that was fine—Dr. Corbin is, for the most part, a good man, a good example for people about how to do right. But—you know, you can't go losing someone without looking back and trying to find the moment you could have made it go the other way, made it not happen— Well. I can't know for sure, but it's hard for me to not see Dr. Corbin's influence as having had an effect—too strong of an effect.

You see, many years ago, when Johnny was just a little boy, I took him up to the zoo because he'd been asking after it for months—then, finally, I got it all together—gas in the car, took a whole Saturday off work to drive up there. But once we were there, he went right up to the lion cage and looks in there for a long while, just thinking, then he sat down on the ground and cried a whole hour, everyone looking at him, complaining. A guard told me we had to move along, that Johnny was upsetting everyone who was here to see the lion, but he wouldn't move. Maybe another parent would have gotten physical with him, but that's not the way I did things—maybe I would have if I could, but I never had the nerve. The lion was pacing at the back of the cage, not looking at anyone. I tried to get Johnny to come along, to go on to the next animal, but he wouldn't. It just about took forever to get out of there and get him in the car to go home, and it wasn't until the end of the summer that he told me what had made him so upset. He said he couldn't see the difference between himself and the lion. And I said, Johnny—*he was maybe eleven or twelve at the time—I said,* Johnny you're a little boy who goes to school and plays sports and sings in the choir and a lion is a lion. *He was a very bright boy—ahead in all his classes, reading without me even asking him to, so I thought he'd understand, but he said—and I'll always remember him saying this, he said—*Ma, they've got eyes like anyone else. *So I told him what I know, which is that a lion's eyes are much bigger than a little boy's eyes, that they're not like his eyes at all, but he wasn't having it. He started listing off all the other animals at the zoo—ones he hadn't even seen—and saying how they weren't any different from him either and he was just so sure about it. It was causing him pain, this idea, it was clearly upsetting him, all those animals locked up, but I didn't know what to do about it. He couldn't be reasoned with. Even as a little boy. He had his ideas and he held them.*

As she spoke, I could feel her both wanting and not wanting

to look into my eyes—my eyes like anyone else's. I sat there within or behind myself, and listened to her speak.

After a little while I thought he'd forgotten about how much the zoo had upset him, and he started reading his Bible a bit more and he just loved Dr. Corbin, wanted to get to Sunday school early all the time . . . and it did make me glad to see him so moved by it all, but also—and I don't know how to say it—he seemed a little . . . upset. He took it all so seriously. Everything seemed to hurt him. All of it, the whole world. Then he wouldn't eat meat, not even fish or anything, then it was eggs and dairy—wouldn't eat those either—and for a while he was even worried about the farmers. Well, there was hardly anything he would eat. He wanted to know who had grown and picked everything I tried to give him— and he got so thin. Fourteen, fifteen years old and smaller than a girl—I didn't know what to do. I took him to doctors, a psychologist all the way up in the city—nothing would work. He was so frail but the hospital wouldn't take him because I didn't have the right insurance—imagine not helping a sick child because of some damn paperwork—and the other doctors just said he was being stubborn, that he'd grow out of it soon. Then Dr. Corbin was no help and anyway he's not even a medical *doctor . . . Sure, people call him doctor but he's no doctor—probably wouldn't know how to operate a Band-Aid. Anyway, I didn't know what to do, and my brother said I was overreacting, said that me caring so much would just make it worse. But I couldn't help it—I could see the bones in his face when I looked at him—like looking at his skeleton. Whose fault would it be if not mine? My son.*

She sat there quietly, pressed her hands flat on the table, then slowly pulled them into her lap.

Well, he did get better, eventually, started eating a little more, though he still wouldn't have meat and if I cooked any of it at home, he would try to have a conversation with it. One time he read a bunch of poems to a package of ground beef on the kitchen counter. Another time he told me he could hear the voices of the dead, people and animals, and they all spoke the same language. Well, I never did know what to say to that. Hearing voices of the dead . . . it didn't even seem particularly Christian.

I felt sure then that I would understand Mrs. Columbus's son and he would understand me and the only tragedy was that he was not here and would never be here again and I knew this was true from the way that sorrow had calcified on Mrs. Columbus. Some things a person cannot help but know.

But Johnny was always serious about his church, and even though I think it was Dr. Corbin who'd gotten Johnny onto being a vegetarian, he was no help with the mess it created for me. He still insists that Johnny chose that path on his own accord, that he never told him what to do. A few years went by, and it seemed Johnny had calmed down a little, so I started asking him about that time—the zoo, the starving, the worrying, speaking to meat. I asked him if he'd maybe been depressed or something, and he told me it was all something he'd received from Scripture. And he said, Ma, I don't deserve anything, maybe others do, but I don't, *so I said,* Johnny, I think you deserve things, *but he said,* No. *Then he said all kinds of things I didn't understand and at the end of it he said he didn't think that Christians were special, that even the Bible had parts that drew lines between people, and now even the church didn't mean anything to him, and he'd only kept going to appease me.*

Mrs. Columbus was looking at the ceiling, shaking her head a little but holding her eyes still.

Well, that was a strange thing to hear as I thought he was the one who had been taking me to church—that I'd been going mostly for his benefit and not really my own. It's true that I had noticed that Johnny hadn't been sitting up at night to read the Bible and he'd stopped leading the prayer at supper and wasn't singing during the church service anymore, but I hadn't wanted to make anything of it. I just felt glad he hadn't moved out after high school, that he wanted to stay close, that he didn't join the military or go off somewhere like other boys did. Then, only a few days before he went away, Johnny kept telling me about how he didn't believe in anyone being different from anyone else, and I told him, well, I agreed with that, that all of God's children are equal and he said, no, not like that. He said it was larger and harder to believe, that he had begun to think you couldn't even love just one person more than someone else, that you couldn't prefer one community over another one, that you couldn't believe in one country over another one, that you couldn't even prefer your own by-blood family—that the family you were born into didn't mean anything, that you couldn't even have a name. You had to give it all up. You had to truly be nothing. He said that's what Jesus was really teaching and all these people had it wrong. You had to be nothing. Nothing.

Mrs. Columbus quickly pressed a handkerchief to her face.

Not even a name. He wouldn't even have his own name. She shook her head. *It wasn't easy, he told me, for him to believe all this, but he also said it was too late for him to not believe it. And when I looked at him, I could see it, too. He wasn't there anymore. No one was there anymore.*

She put the handkerchief back into her purse. She looked at me closely and slowly.

So. You can see why . . . when I heard about some young person being found in that other church I thought, well . . . maybe. But you're not. I know you're not him. I don't know you at all.

She looked at me one last time and I looked at her and what she said was simply not true. We did know each other. Whatever we may have known before or since didn't matter. Even as she said she didn't know me, I could see this and I felt sure that she could, too. It didn't matter what was said, not this time. A word is put down as a placeholder for something that cannot be communicated, no matter what anyone tries, no matter how many words accumulate, there is always that absence. I stayed silent.

Well, I stopped going to church and it's true I may have said some cross things to Dr. Corbin since Johnny left, but he must know that he owes me my son. He must know that much.

Dr. Corbin had come back in and was standing near us. Mrs. Columbus stood and turned to look at him.

Everyone thinks that bad things only happen in a place like Almose County and nothing bad happens here, she said. *But they're wrong. They're all wrong.*

I listened to her steps retreating, away from us and never to come back. Dr. Corbin sat again. Someone brought over two blue plates heavy with stewed vegetables and we ate them, not even stopping to look at each other.

DR. CORBIN SLOWED THE TRUCK when he saw someone walking on the road ahead of us. The walking person wore a wide-brimmed hat and wasn't carrying anything, their arms hanging as if only attached but otherwise unaffiliated with the rest of the body.

Where you headed? Dr. Corbin called out as we reached him.

Ain't in any hurry to get there, the man said back.

Very good, Dr. Corbin said. *Take care now, you hear?*

Oh, you can bet I will.

We drove on.

The road we'd been following, thick green fields on either side, curved into another road and led us into a neighborhood of slight, stooped houses. A fire hydrant was spewing on one corner and several children jumped in and out of the stream, their clothes soaked and heavy on them.

It's a special day, the day before the festival . . . with the kids out of school and all, you have to do something with them.

He parked the car in front of a small yellow house with no trees around it.

Suppose that's part of the reason they sent you over here. Everyone over there is supposed to stay inside all day, to get ready, I suppose.

The air was heavy and warm. We walked into the house,

not much cooler, but all the lights were off. Dr. Corbin was carrying a paper sack he set down on the edge of a couch.

We haven't got a spare room, so you'll have to sleep here if that's all right. Well, even if it ain't all right, that's what we've got. He smiled. *Hilda sent this bag of clothes with you—she said you might need a change of clothes.* He shrugged and we went out the back door of the house to a yard where several people were gathered in white folding chairs around tables draped with bright blue cloths. A child ran up to me and grabbed my hand and led me to a small dogwood tree in the corner of the fenced yard. Three or four dogs were chasing one another and sniffing the ground in search of something.

Look! the child said, pointing at the tree. A doll was bent over a branch just out of reach, hair flung the wrong way over her head. *She's stuck up there*, the child said seriously, then ran toward one of the dogs, singing as she went.

A familiar voice behind me—*I figured a church would get you eventually.* It was the woman from the gas station, the one that had given me milk and whiskey.

You go on and get yourself something to eat, you hear? Got to save up your energy this time of year, and the heat being like it is. You got to save up your resources.

She pointed toward a table covered in plates and large bowls and cakes caving into the spaces where slices had been cut. Someone was shouting at Dr. Corbin there, trying to force a small plate of something into his hands.

Nice to see your sweet face, baby, the woman from the gas station said. *I never seen a face as sweet as yours.* She looked in my eyes, calm and inspecting. *You take care, now, bye-bye.*

A part of the yard sloped down and there a long, narrow tarp had been laid down, and a hose was running water across it. Children flung themselves down it, one or two at once, on their bellies, face-first, screaming.

You going to give it a try? Dr. Corbin asked, appearing at my elbow. He handed me a piece of cake on a plate. *These ladies won't rest until you've had some cake, so you may as well go on and have it. No arguing with them. No, sir.*

He and I sat in some chairs beneath a tree too sparse to give shade. People came up to talk to Dr. Corbin, sometimes to pray with him, sometimes just to tell him things. Mostly Dr. Corbin said little in reply. He listened, nodded, his mouth making small smiles that came and went. Sometimes someone would pat my shoulder or say something to me, too, and all the while I thought about the way that stained-glass light bleeds onto the ceiling in those first moments of a morning, spilled and soft. Hardly anyone ever sees it, I thought, and I wondered if Mrs. Columbus had ever seen it or whether Johnny or Dr. Corbin had.

Come here and let me look at you. Someone was standing near, someone large. I looked up, half-shielding my eyes from the sun's glint—a bright red shirt and a patchy black beard.

This is Leonard, Dr. Corbin said to me.

OK, Leonard said, bending his knees with trouble to stoop at my chair. *All right, here we go.* He looked right at me with hardly a feeling to see in his face at all. *You been here since Sunday?*

Yes, Dr. Corbin said, though Leonard had only been looking at me. A woman was at Dr. Corbin's side, discreetly crying and explaining something sad about someone she loved.

Hm, Leonard said. *I imagine we were the last stop, were we? Hm. They had to send you over here because they didn't know what to do with you? Or they got tired of doing it? That's how it is? I see. I see how it is. That's how they're going to be—and this week on top of everything—today on top of everything. Well. I see how it is. I see.*

The Reverend over at the church on Main Street called up and asked me to help out, Dr. Corbin said. *And I said we didn't mind—I don't mind at least.*

Suppose we don't mind! Leonard said. *On top of everything right now, we got to help them out whenever they ask, is that how it is?*

The woman crying at Dr. Corbin's side began to cry a little less discreetly, still whispering something to him through her tears as a mass of children across the lawn screamed in pleasure in the water in the heat.

And who was this kid staying with over there? Leonard asked.

The Bonner family.

And who's the lady of that house?

Hilda Bonner.

Gladstone, though. She's a Gladstone.

I don't know anything about it, Dr. Corbin said.

You ought to though. It's what I'd been hearing about from Maize. She said last Sunday this family came into her place after church last week because, you know, since last year all these white people come over to her place for their Sunday dinner now. I don't know why. They must have all agreed about it. I don't know. But Maize knows Hilda since she used to look after her when she was a little girl until she got word about who Mr. Gladstone was, then she quit real quick.

And so, what—what are you saying? Dr. Corbin asked.

I'm not saying we shouldn't help someone who needs help. But to be honest I don't quite know what to think about the whole thing only that it don't sit right with me. Maize found out from her sister they found the kid sleeping in their church and they take it upon themselves to be the saviors, to take the kid in and try to figure something out on their own—don't even alert child services or nothing, which I know because I know some people who work over there and I looked in on it—then they give up once it gets too complicated, that is, when half of them start saying maybe the kid's not white or not white enough and then what happens, huh? What do they do then? They want to make it our problem. They think it's time we did something about it. That or maybe Hilda's daddy found out what she was up to and wasn't having it—

Now, I don't know about that, Dr. Corbin said. The weeping woman was no longer weeping, her eyes closed, one hand thumbing a beaded bracelet in the other.

I'm just calling it like I see it. It's just all the timing of it the moment they pick to send him over here, you see?

He? the woman who had been crying asked in a tiny voice. *I really—well, I thought—*

He, she, or she or he—it don't matter to me, Leonard said, louder now, *I don't care. It don't make a bit of difference—*

Y'all shush now, talking like that, all kinds of rude, a woman said, leaning toward Leonard as she stood near.

What am I going to say or not say in front of this kid? Leonard asked her.

We don't know who this child is, that's all. We shouldn't be treating them like—

We sure don't. Leonard's voice flattened hers. *And if he'd showed up on his own volition here, it would be one thing, but they got sent over here by a Gladstone.*

A Gladstone? That Gladstone?

There ain't any other Gladstone families except the one.

Oh, the woman said. *Well, I don't know anything about that.*

Everybody knows who he is, Leonard said, seeming to speak to everyone. *Everybody knows and nobody says. Isn't that always the way? Everyone knowing and nobody saying.*

The woman had turned to leave but looked over her shoulder to ask, *Didn't they put him away somewhere finally?*

That's what I heard, yes. And now his daughter sent this kid over here on this day of all the days. And no one sees any trouble with it.

You know as well as I do that the Gladstones did a lot for our community. Donated all sorts of—

But everybody knows what else he did and nobody says, Leonard said.

And he paid for Luella's daughter's wedding since she couldn't, Dr. Corbin said. *Paid for the whole thing out of his own pocket.*

And you know what else he paid for—paid off the sheriff, that's what. Everyone knows it's true. Used to be anybody could get out of jail free if you're on the right side of Mr. Gladstone. The sheriff still calls up Gladstone to ask him about this or that, is this guy all right or isn't he, that kind of thing. I know somebody in the department is why I know. She hears all his phone calls and he underestimates her, that's what—

Well, I don't know anything about that, Dr. Corbin said.

Doesn't seem anyone knows quite enough about it.

Dr. Corbin was turning a book over in his hands. The others

fell quiet, then spoke among themselves for a while. Someone said something about *personal fortitude* and someone else said, *Oh, here he goes with the personal fortitude again.* I don't remember Leonard leaving, but he must have gone away, scattered with the others back into their homes, their lives. There was, it seemed, so much to look after.

The sky shifted and the light shifted. The dogs were all sleeping in the shade of the house. The hose had been turned off and the children all sat on the ground, eating or napping or making little mounds out of the mud. Dr. Corbin was carrying things back into the house, stopping now and then to wipe his forehead with a white bandanna.

I turned to see someone sitting in the chair beside mine—an old woman wearing a bright blue suit, a hat with a tiny feather tucked in a ribbon at the brim. When she removed the hat, I could see the way her face had been shattered by time—something acidic and clean about her eyes, washed-out and elsewhere. It seemed a bright light had faded everything they'd ever seen, gifted them with emptiness.

We knew you'd come, she said. *We just knew it.*

In one hand she held her hat and in the other, a cane—the handle was a rabbit's head, polished cherrywood, gleaming gem for an eye.

Our new jesus.

She tapped the cane on the ground and smiled her tiny teeth.

All this time we spent waiting and being called foolish. We never been foolish, we know, just faithful. And I knew it, knew it all along, knew this happy day would be upon just us given enough time. I thank our Lord I lived to see it.

She nodded.

Now, tell me, how long'd you know? Did you know the whole time or did it only occur to you lately?

I said nothing but she squinted at me and shook her head as if I were speaking to her, as if she were listening to a large, important story.

And how'd you find out about it? Did he come to you and tell you direct?

She stared into my eyes and I stared into hers. Such a prone and open tenderness, one I'd never seen or known before. I did not blink. I did not move.

Well, I'll be. . . . It's quite a story, ain't it? What a life our God has given us. To be this close to it all. To be this close. In all things, we trust you. In all things, we follow you. We follow you to the end.

She and I sat there quietly for a while.

One last day. One last sunset. She shook her head. Her smile was so broadly held I could nearly hear its silent laughter. *All this, all of this is leaving now. All of us, your children, we're leaving now. All the birds are going to die. All the dogs, all the unbaptized, all the worms and beetles. Begin again. Something new. Maybe nothing. Nothing at all forever. It was all for this, wasn't it? It was all for this now. This last day.*

She looked out calmly for a while and the light kept shifting on us, then, seeming to forget me completely and still watching the wind barely fluttering the dogwood branches, she said, *Did I ever tell you what I think about it? What I think is—what the problem is—what the real problem of it all is—they ought to stop all their fuss. I know they mean well, or some of them at least mean well, but they all ought to stop calling themselves something—you know? Religion, yes. Clergy, no. That's what I say.*

Mama, take this, a younger man said, handing her a few white pills and a cup of water. She brought her shaking hand up to her mouth and the water spilled from the cup, dampened her lap, but her eyes never unsteadied, not for a moment.

THE COUCH HAD BEEN MADE UP like a bed, the sheets tucked into the cushions, pillow there, folded quilt there. A woman standing beside Dr. Corbin was smiling with a hidden intensity. *We're so glad you're here*, she said, her arms coming toward me, then around me, the warmth of her body coming near then against mine. She held me like that awhile and warm tears from her face fell down my neck, down the back of my shirt, cooling on my skin, dampening the cloth, sinking into me.

Now that's enough, Dr. Corbin said, *we ought to let Pew get some rest now, don't you think so?* She detached from me and I could see how reddened her eyes had become, as if she were allergic to me. A phone rang and she moved quickly into the kitchen to answer it.

Binnie's a good woman, Dr. Corbin said, looking toward the kitchen. We heard her speaking into the phone, her voice concerned and intent. *But she gets overwhelmed by other people—she has to be careful of that. Taking care of others. It takes something, you know, it takes something from you to take care of another person and there's only so much a person has to give.*

It's Randall, she called out from the kitchen.

See now, here we go, Dr. Corbin whispered to me, then shouted, *Oh, and how's he doing?*

Just needs a place for the night—

Oh, does he?

I said I'd ask you.

Suppose it's all right. We've got the other couch if Pew don't mind.

I nodded. *Pew don't mind*, Dr. Corbin called out. *Suppose it's all right then.*

He's my nephew, Binnie said as she came back into the living room with a pile of folded sheets and quilts. *And from time to time my sister sends him out. They have these disagreements. He's had trouble finding work.*

More like keeping it, Dr. Corbin said. Binnie sent her eyes at him in a tiny, quick way, then aimed them back at her task of laying blankets and sheets on the couch. *You can't say it ain't true.*

He's a good young man.

Ain't so young anymore.

He's young on the inside. Binnie's tone shifted, her eyes heavier. *He has a young heart.*

Yes. Yes, he does.

I lay on one of the couches and covered myself with the blankets.

You're just going to sleep in your clothes like that, Dr. Corbin said, *are you?*

I looked up at him to say yes without saying yes. He smiled. *Makes getting up a little faster, don't it?*

A while later, Dr. Corbin was gone and only Binnie was there, standing by the front window, waiting until Randall came in wearing a plaid pajama set and dirty slippers.

I thank you, Aunt Binnie, I do thank you.

No need to thank me. You have a roommate this time. Did you hear?

That's what I heard.

This is Randall, Binnie said, announcing him to the room.

Nice to meet you, Randall said, a hand extended toward me. I slipped my arm from the quilts and took his hand, was shaken by it.

Now you let Pew sleep, you hear? Don't go talking all night like you do. Everyone needs a good night's sleep, you know. And Pew's going to the festival.

Oh, is that right?

Yessir, now you get to sleep.

All right, now, all right, Randall said, pulling the quilt up to his chin as Binnie left us, turning out the lights as she went. I lay in the dark silence awhile, aware of another body, a stranger's body, in the room with me, a comfort both far off and nearby. I could not hear him breathing but I knew he was. The air in the room moved differently from how it had when I slept in that attic room.

The way I see it, some people just live slower than others is all. His voice cut through the dark and silent room. *Mama says I've reached an age that I have to do this thing or that thing and I don't want to do either and she said it's a problem. I don't think so but she does think so. She said she can't stand to have me at home another minute. I think her mood might change. She misses me when I'm not there, that's what she says anyway, so I come over here sometimes, then I go back. Her own son still at home and it makes her sad is what she said.* I'm only thirty-five, *I said, and she said,* Only thirty-five! *I don't see it as that old. I think I live slower.*

I think I might live to two hundred. People used to and I think I might start it again.

Randall, Binnie's voice called from the bedroom. *Now quit it, will you? Pew ain't trying to talk to you. Everybody needs to sleep right about now so get to it.*

Yes, ma'am, he said, reverent and quiet. The bedroom door shut. The house became still and more still and stiller still.

Can I ask you something? he whispered after some time had passed.

Yes, I whispered back.

How old are you?

I can't remember.

It's better that way—his voice was getting lost and sleepy—*it's better you don't ever know. You could live a long life that way. You could probably grow up slower if you don't know. You know, I do a lot with my time, I really do. I spend a lot of time thinking about things. Like how if you look at a word for long enough or if you say the same word over and over, it starts to sound crazy, or it starts to not even sound like a word or not even look like a word. I spend a lot of time thinking about that.*

An appliance in the kitchen began to buzz.

It's making ice. Aunt Binnie got her one of those kinds of freezers that makes the ice. It used to scare me when I slept over but I know it now. It can't scare you if you know it's going to happen. But then there's all kinds of things we don't know that are going to happen. And so it's scary sometimes, I think it is, scary to have to go around out there. They told me you don't live anywhere and I find it hard to believe. I don't know how a person could do that. It's confusing. It's that feeling, that feeling of staring at a word

189

for so long it's not a word anymore. I don't ever want my mother to go away.

He was silent for a long time.

Nobody's mother should ever not be there, but my mother told me all mothers eventually are not there. I can't understand it. I don't even want to.

We slept.

SATURDAY

I woke when the house was still dark and silent, a morning sky just beginning to brighten at the windows. Randall was gone. The quilts and sheets he'd slept on were folded neatly, stacked at the edge of the couch. I went to the front porch and watched clouds that never made good on the threat of rain. Light was beginning to flicker through when Binnie came out with her hair held back in a pale yellow cloth. She set a cup of coffee down beside me, wordless, and went back inside. Sometime later Dr. Corbin brought out to me the brown paper sack that Hilda had given him and emptied it on the table. A dress, a pair of pants, a pair of stockings, two thin shirts (each of them missing buttons), two pairs of clean socks, and a thick white bathrobe.

I guess you're s'posed to take your pick, Dr. Corbin said, looking at the clothes. *The robe—that's useful though—you'll need that today.*

The bathrobe had a few little holes at the seam of one sleeve. I stood, put myself inside the robe, tied the white sash around my body, and sat down again. Dr. Corbin sat, too, each of us drinking that bitter coffee, listening to birds.

It starts in a few hours, he said after some time had passed between us. *You know—I was a part of the group that started it all those years ago, started the festival. And I believed it was what we all needed—I believed in it then. Now, though, I can't say I am altogether sure I understand what it does to people . . . I felt so sure then—of course I was younger. It's easier to be certain of things then—and the older you get, the more you see how certainty depends on one blindness or another.*

A bird landed on the railing and Dr. Corbin stopped talking to look at him. The bird turned his head one way, then the other. He stooped, widened his wings, and went away.

Forgiveness is sometimes just a costume for forgetting. I don't want it to be so—but every year, just before it begins, I start to feel this way. And then what? I forget about it.

In the street several policemen marched by, dressed in white and carrying white guns.

Hey there, little possum, Dr. Corbin said to a girl sprinting up the stairs.

I'm not a possum! She climbed into his lap. *Mama told me to come over here.* She stood on his knees and took his ears in each of her little hands.

Why are your ears so big?

So I can hear when a little possum sneaks up on me, Dr. Corbin said.

Who is that?

This is our friend Pew.

Why does she look like that? Her voice lowered as she turned away from me.

Dr. Corbin gave no answer, picked up the child, and went inside, calling out for Binnie, telling her a little possum called

JJ had come by looking for breakfast. The door shut, and for a few minutes I could hear the muted sounds of lives being passed inside the house—a chime of fork on plate, doors opened or shut, words muffled through walls.

I'm not sure what I can even explain about it, Dr. Corbin said as he joined me on the porch again. *It became something I didn't mean for it to be . . . maybe it means something to them that keep doing it—I don't know. I guess Steven already told you what you need to know—and anyway, I guess you'll see when you're there. There's hardly any use in explaining it. It's a ritual. We make them, people make them, and they don't really mean anything, even the ones that supposedly mean something—even they don't really mean anything. They're just something to do.*

A white police car drove by slowly; Dr. Corbin waved.

Well, I guess I ought to take you that direction about now.

On the drive I saw families on the sidewalks in white, girls in white dresses and white stockings, white suits on the fathers, mothers draped in white. White hats and white shoes. Someone pushed a wheelchair that held someone draped with a white blanket, and boys were in white short pants, babies were swaddled in white, white vests were over white shirts, white scarves.

A few white trucks carried children in their beds. On the back of one truck was a sign, red letters on white—

ALL LIVING THINGS

ARE BROKEN THINGS

A large group of boys all together carried one wide sign—

> ALL FAILURES
> ARE FORGIVEN

And a group of girls carried another behind them—

> ALL FAILURES
> ARE FORGOTTEN

We're here, Dr. Corbin said. *Just follow the crowd where they go. I can't drive up any closer. I'll meet you right here once it's over.* I looked at him for a while. It was hard to feel as if I'd ever see anyone again. The day was peeled back like that, something raw and ending.

The crowd was all walking in the same direction, a synchronized flood. Small children and babies hung in the arms of the larger people, unaware and unable, and a spare cough or sneeze sometimes broke through the warm silence, as the body has its ways to speak without speaking.

The crowd become more dense, slower. The trucks rolled along with us. Church bells were ringing and sirens sang in the distance as we approached a large dark building in the center of the parking lot. Above a doorway wide enough for many cattle to pass through, a large flap of canvas hung—

> MAY WE FORGET
> ALL WE FORGIVE

Just inside the entrance, children were being left in a large room full of children, some weeping, some gleeful, most sitting bored and quiet on the floor. In a glimpse I saw a few women—some pregnant, some carrying a baby in each arm—moving among the crawling and mumbling children. I kept in step with the crowd as we went deeper into the building. No one looked into anyone's eyes. The silence became more silent, more silent still.

At the end of the hallway—a massive space. The ceiling was higher than any church I'd ever known. The tall windows on one side of the room were fogged with dark soot, and the walls were the color of molasses, and the wooden floor creaked with our steps. Wide ceiling fans spun above us. The robe I'd almost forgotten had come slightly undone. I tightened it. Some people were taking others by the shoulders and leading them to specific points around the room, putting them in some kind of formation. A set of hands guided me to a spot and set me there.

Through the crowd, in profile, I saw Hilda in a white dress. Her face looked smaller and softer and less clear than I remembered. I wondered what she would say, but I didn't want to hear her say it. Did she feel she'd wronged or been wronged more in her life? Did anyone ever know which was true? How much harm did we cause without knowing it? How much harm did we cause when we were certain we were doing such good?

Something about the way Hilda's hair had been tightly contained on the back of her head made me feel the pressure and presence of every person who had never been born, and even in this large room nearly full and still filling with people, even in this crowd, I felt that infinite crowd, all those other selves that both existed and did not exist, lives both impossible, unborn, never born, and still present.

The few lights in the room, already dim, grew dimmer. Baskets of black scarves were passed around. Everyone took a scarf, tied it over their eyes, and through the crowd I noticed Nelson watching everyone do this, before doing the same—covering his eyes and letting his arms go slack at his sides. Young men at the edge of the room pulled on ropes as pulleys above us creaked, and wide white curtains came down, separating some people from others, grouping some of us together, creating soft hallways and rooms within this room. The air in the room tightened, seemed to resist my lungs. I tied the scarf over my eyes as everyone else had. The shuffling of the crowd stilled, then stilled more. I heard the fans shut off, a solidity taking over, then a bell sounding several times.

Many voices began at once—some I seemed to know, some I almost remembered, some I could have remembered, some I did not know, some I thought I did not know, some I recognized, some that sounded like my own, some that seemed to belong to people long lost to me, some that sounded like people I would later know or one day become—but the words were unintelligible at first, too far away or spoken too quickly, too softly, too warped. People began to move, the steps tentative at first, then faster, hands held out to blunt the meeting of one body against another, shoulders lightly knocking together, feet stepping on feet then correcting themselves.

I've been lying //
        Cheated on last year's //
                with her for several months //
        may have taken //

Half sentences or full sentences, men's and women's voices,
defiant or sorrowful, spoken quickly, spoken slowly, they came
like a chorus, shared a sort of cadence—

I don't tithe as much as //   *judge them //*
        I cheated on //
    charge blacks more so they won't //
given bribes to some at the //
            not sure I've ever been grateful //
                    my brother's lawn mower and sold it //
        dream of divorce //   I take everything for granted //
she would die sooner rather than later //
        I judge them //   not sure I believe in God //
I beat that little girl //   people at the courthouse //
don't want to help them //
            I cheated on my algebra //
        still haven't told him yet //   I'm not sure I love my wife //
I stole groceries when I was //
        for some months I regretted having the baby //
passing judgment //   I've been testing God all year //
I killed her pony because we couldn't afford to //
                    took cash from her purse //
curse every day // I hit her sometimes // won't stop watching porn //

really don't like reading the Bible but I pretend //
I never want to go to church //
    I shot three squirrels for no reason //   killed some //
real drunk and lied about it //

              strongly covet my neighbor's // hate the festival //
My business partners don't know I take more //
    feeding him expired chicken salad on purpose //
Might not tell him ever //

     know I did not pay //   don't like the looks of them //
         hate this time of year //
   slash their tires in the parking lot //
never ask forgiveness //   why can't I hate them //
   lie all the time about everything // said I didn't have any //
     I stole my sister's clothes and threw them out //
I saw a murder and //

    take the Lord's name in vain //   I know who did //
   I want a divorce //   don't want to pay taxes for the //
can't manage to forgive //

    all year I've wanted to run away // but I'm lazy //
      I watch pornography //
     really do hate her and can't stop //
didn't really hear God's voice when I said I did //

             I take more than my //

   she thinks I'm clean //
told my wife I was on business when //   pay for sex //
  don't want to give money to the poor // don't trust //
not sure if the Bible really tells us that all men are //
     what if there's just no God //

I resist my husband //   I'm glad he's dead //
we were both drunk //   I despise the new preacher //
   it's a struggle to believe // I steal money from my father's //
no one knows that I'm the one who //
   I wish I was dead // made up speaking in //
don't love my children equally // I lied //
   I hide my money because //
afraid everyone can tell that she's not //
   never actually read the Bible //
      women and can't figure why I shouldn't //
I have been sleeping with one of //
   lied to //   I'm not really sure the festival is //
I know I'm not fair to // can't stop being glad he's gone //
want to have sex with almost anyone but my husband //
   I do not want to forgive him //   premarital //
      cries every day at her desk and I pretend not to hear //
   dug up my neighbor's tulip bulbs //
   a beer this morning //   I wish I was dead //
might never forgive him //
   every year I try to figure out who said what //
      blame them //
forced her to //
      pretended I didn't know why they didn't bloom //
   hate this stupid thing and //   I threatened him //
I don't think I'll ever really forgive her //   even right now //
   take bribes all the //   proud and vain //
I've tried to kill myself twice //   made her do //
   feel sad that people need there to be a God just to be good to //

Several bells starting chiming and the voices—some of them moving faster now, some of them choked with crying, some of them angry—began to splinter, fade, cease.

> *don't know how to stop hating her //*
> *don't always think God's creation is //*
> *I know I killed //*
> *I doubt all the time //*
> *took a magazine from the doctor's //*
> *not sure I can stop //*

The bells drowned out the voices, washed them away, then the last bells sounded and the last sounds hummed and dissolved. Someone put a hand in mine—*I forgive you. I forgive you*, someone else said, shaking my hand again. *I forgive you*, said another, then another. Hands came into mine, and every hand felt both exactly the same and completely different. Everyone was forgiving everyone. I removed the scarf from my eyes to see some faces reddened, tear wet, some drained white in fear. Some kept their scarves on. Some people weren't moving at all. Some weren't saying anything. Just beyond the rumble of all this forgiveness I could hear every child in town, crying, their sorrow roaring like heavy rain, a storm of it.

Children—they know sin so well and they know God so well, a voice behind me said. I turned. It was one of the women I'd seen in the kitchen the other day. *They know greed and love more than adults remember. They know God; they know terror. Know it by instinct. All the growing up is to forget what we know at birth. Ain't it true? They cry because they can't confess—know their wickedness but can't say it. That's why they cry. But don't you worry—they'll quiet down eventually.*

She walked away from me. Others laughed or covered their faces. Some lay on the floor and some stood, holding one another. Some seemed not to be moving at all, not looking at anything, not thinking of anything. They were not anywhere, not anyplace at all. The lights were slowly brightening back on, and the curtains were being raised. The fans began spinning, humming above us, and the children came running in throughout the room, looking up at everyone from knee level, looking for a place to belong, for the person that would pick the child up.

At the edge of the room I saw Tammy crouched on the floor, and Hal stooped over her, covering her, holding her still. She was moaning, shaking, covering her face.

Some years you just hear too much is all, Hal was explaining to someone nearby. I felt relieved he didn't see me passing by. I didn't want either of them to remember me, to know I'd been here, that I'd gone through this time with them. A numbed feeling had overtaken the room and I didn't want it to touch me.

A town has a feeling, I remembered someone telling me long ago, because certain kinds of thought are contagious. I'd never known exactly what that meant and maybe I still do not know, but I think I came to know it then.

Amen, a voice said. *Amen.* It was everywhere, all at once, like sunlight.

Where is the voice coming from? a child asked, but the adult standing above the child didn't answer, held a finger over her mouth. The voice began to list names—*Edward*—and slowly the crowd fell silent again—*Earl*—listening to them as if listening to music—*Johnson*.

What are they doing now? the same child asked.

Reading the names, the adult whispered back.

Whose names?

Of the dead.

All the dead?

Some of them.

Which ones?

The adult hesitated. The child listened intently, as if she might be able to decode what was happening. She stared at the ceiling. She was learning how to live.

Which ones? she whispered again.

The ones who were killed.

Today?

No, not today. In years past.

Oh.

The names that had no holders kept coming.

Why did they die?

We all do.

But they were killed?

Yes.

Will we all be killed?

No.

Then why were they killed?

The adult was quiet for a little while longer, then knelt beside the child.

Because of what they might have done.

Who killed them?

The people we elected.

Do all elected people have to kill people?

Yes.

Why would anyone want to get elected?

Someone has to be elected, the adult said after some time. *We have to elect people.*

And why are they reading their names?

Because it's the sin we've all done together. Something we had to do even though it was evil.

Even me?

I don't know. Maybe not you. Not yet.

The child sat on the floor. Her face needed to be washed with tears, warm water from the body, the body's way of saying, *Yes, I am still in here.*

When the last name was read, the voice said, *Amen,* and everyone said, *Amen.*

A picnic, the voice said, would be served in the parking lot, and the crowd moved peacefully toward the doors we'd come in through, but at the back of the room I saw an open door and just beyond it the moving shadow of someone who had just passed through it. When I looked around for anyone who might be accounting for me, all I could see was that numbness, no one seeing anyone, everyone walking away from here in the same direction.

I walked toward the back door. I stepped outside. The storm of people's voices faded behind me. Annie was standing there, looking out toward the fields that stretched far from us, went places it seemed we might never go. A few others were there, too, their faces not numbed, just still. Air sat between us all like it will sit between anyone. The sky didn't know one of us from the other.

What are we supposed to do now? Annie asked someone, perhaps me or herself or you.

Far from us trees were gathered in twos and threes. I knew I wasn't supposed to be here. It was all an accident. All of us were meant to be somewhere else. I stood and walked away, and once I was one step away from her, I was as alone as I had ever been but I also knew that Annie—this Annie who answers to Annie but who has another, truer name—I knew she was not lost to the world just because she was lost to this place. She and I were deeper inside the world now, farther inside the dirt, braided into your vocal cords, the ones hanging in your throat.

No one knows where I went, and I don't know where I went and I don't know where Annie went or where you went, but I know that I went and was gone and was gone completely. That night, all was quiet, and all is still quiet. All is uncertain. Gray clouds churned overhead—and still they churn, still they cast shadows, will cast them long after we're all gone. The ground is wet. I was alone then and I've been alone ever since. All of us are gone and were gone and have been gone forever.

All is quiet now; the sky is uncertain. I am moving, perhaps I am moving toward you. The ground is gray and the sky is wet. I am uncertain. The ground is not uncertain. I am not alone; I am with the sky and ground and you are with another sky, another ground. Is this ours now? The sky is certain and the wet is certain and I am quiet. Will we find each other? The ground is silent. I am uncertain. The sky is quiet. It's never known any of us from the other. We speak with borrowed air. The sky only seems to be blue and have an edge.

BE ADVISED

Emily Bell and Eric Chinski frequently disregard national borders, guiding people and supplies across them. Jin Auh drives an armored truck through hopeless, pitch-dark streets. Brian Gittis, Julia Ringo, Jackson Howard, Alba Bailey-Zigler, Ekin Oklap, and their many dangerous associates are not to be underestimated and could be leading a sizable revolution at this very moment. The Whiting Foundation and the University of Mississippi provided meals, medical care, and a canvas tent. Kathleen Alcott and Brenda Cullerton practice obscure forms of sorcery.

Flannery O'Connor, Zora Neale Hurston, Carson McCullers, and Eudora Welty have been robbed. Ursula K. Le Guin is a high priestess of the universe. David Buckel walked away from Omelas. "Derek Parfit" mattered.

Jesse Ball is a mysterious weather pattern that has never been directly observed and can only be measured by its aftermath.

Catherine Lacey is the author of the novels *Nobody Is Ever Missing* and *The Answers* and the short-story collection *Certain American States*. She has received a Guggenheim Fellowship, a Whiting Award, and a New York Foundation for the Arts Fellowship. She was a finalist for the New York Public Library's Young Lions Fiction Award and was named one of *Granta*'s Best of Young American Novelists. Her essays and short fiction have appeared in *The New Yorker, Harper's Magazine, The New York Times, The Believer*, and other publications. Born in Mississippi, she is based in Chicago.